## ABOUT THE AUTHORS

**Janelle Denison** is a *USA TODAY* bestselling author of more than fifty contemporary romance novels. She is a two-time recipient of the National Readers' Choice Award, and has also been nominated for the prestigious RITA® Award. Janelle is a California native who now calls Oregon home. She resides in the Portland area with her husband and daughters, and can't imagine a more beautiful place to live. To learn more about Janelle and her upcoming releases, you can visit her website at www.janelledenison.com, or you can chat with her on her group blog at www.plotmonkeys.com.

**Leslie Kelly** has written dozens of books and novellas for the Harlequin Blaze, Temptation and HQN lines. Known for her sparkling dialogue, fun characters and depth of emotion, her books have been honored with numerous awards, including a National Readers' Choice Award, an *RT Book Reviews* Award, and three nominations for the highest award in romance, the RITA® Award. Leslie resides in Maryland with her own romantic hero, Bruce, and their three daughters. Visit her online at www.lesliekelly.com or on her group blog, www.plotmonkeys.com.

**Jo Leigh** lives in a small, small town in Utah with a gorgeous view. She has far too many pets, but they do help to keep her sane and happy. A triple RITA® Award finalist, Jo has written more than fifty novels for Harlequin Books. She also enjoys researching her novels a little too much. The best place to catch her is on Twitter where she's Jo_Leigh, or you can write to her at joleigh@joleigh.com.

# Janelle Denison
# Leslie Kelly, Jo Leigh

## NOT ANOTHER BLIND DATE...

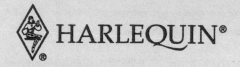

### HARLEQUIN®

TORONTO • NEW YORK • LONDON
AMSTERDAM • PARIS • SYDNEY • HAMBURG
STOCKHOLM • ATHENS • TOKYO • MILAN • MADRID
PRAGUE • WARSAW • BUDAPEST • AUCKLAND

ISBN-13: 978-0-373-79595-6

NOT ANOTHER BLIND DATE...
Copyright © 2011 by Harlequin Books S.A.

The publisher acknowledges the copyright holders of the individual works as follows:

SKIN DEEP
Copyright © 2011 by Janelle Denison

HOLD ON
Copyright © 2011 by Leslie Kelly

EX MARKS THE SPOT
Copyright © 2011 by Jolie Kramer

Recycling programs for this product may not exist in your area.

# CONTENTS

# SKIN DEEP
## Janelle Denison

To Brenda Chin, for always welcoming me back.
To my Plotmonkey Pal, Leslie Kelly—
Thank you for the invite! And to Don—
Thank you for the best twenty-four years of my life!

## 1

SEX WITH A STRANGER was a fantasy Jayne Young had often entertained in her mind while she lay in bed at night, but she never in her wildest dreams would have believed that such a fanciful illusion would *ever* become reality.

She'd always been a quintessential good girl who took things slowly with a guy, and she'd never been tempted to indulge in a one-night stand with any man she'd dated. Yet here she was, allowing a gorgeous, smoldering hot pirate she'd met only a few hours ago to lead her away from the crush of people packed into the nightclub—all of whom were dressed in various costumes for Halloween—to somewhere more secluded where they could be alone and finally give in to the lust that had been simmering between them since the moment their gazes had met from across the room.

In a club full of scantily clad costumed women, she'd been surprised that he'd singled her out. With a slow, devastatingly sexy smile on his lips, he'd strolled toward her, a dashing figure in a billowing white cotton shirt that was halfway unbuttoned and gave every woman in the place a glimpse of his well-defined chest and washboard abs. Tight black breeches molded to his lean hips and hard, muscular thighs, and a royal blue sash cinched his waist.

He'd completed the look of a rogue with his tousled dark brown hair, and a black patch covering one eye. The other was a piercing shade of blue that made her heart flutter in her chest and raised the level of awareness thrumming through her veins.

Stopping before her, he'd executed a gallant, charming bow, his manner reminiscent of Orlando Bloom in *The Pirates of The Caribbean.* "You must be Jane."

That he knew her name had initially startled her, until she realized he was referring to the formfitting, one-shouldered, leopard print mini dress her best friend Darcie, had coaxed her into wearing in hopes of bringing out Jayne's wilder side for the evening. The sexy costume, complete with four-inch leopard print heels and a necklace of faux tiger teeth, had been an amusing and deliberate twist on her own name.

Darcie had glammed up her hair and make-up in hopes that Plain Jayne would find her Tarzan at the club. But even though her character's counter part was nowhere to be found, Jayne was sure her friend would be thrilled to know her efforts to transform Jayne had attracted such a smoking-hot hunk.

"I am Jayne," she replied, raising her voice above the loud music. It didn't matter that he believed she was playing a role—in fact, she preferred it that way. In this sexually charged environment, dressed so provocatively and way outside her personal comfort zone, she liked the fact that she was able to maintain her anonymity.

He straightened, then inclined his head and offered his hand in a sweeping gesture. "Care to take a whirl on the dance floor with a swashbuckling pirate?" he drawled.

She found his attempt to persuade her irresistible, and

the seductive look on his handsome face triggered a jolt of excitement unlike anything she'd ever felt before. Since Darcie had been enticed out onto the dance floor by a vampire, Jayne figured she might as well have some fun, too.

Exhaling a deep breath, she placed her hand in his. "I'd love to join you."

He gave her a flirtatious grin that made her stomach do a little flip, then led her into the throng of costumed revelers who were dancing without inhibition or modesty—a brash and bold attitude that Jayne didn't have much experience with. The atmosphere was electric, and for the first time in her life she threw caution, and her more reserved nature, aside and let herself enjoy the inviting beat of the music, and the pirate who'd picked her out of all the other women in the club.

It didn't take her long to get drawn into the suggestive scene around her, and since she didn't know anyone at the club other than Darcie, it was easy to relax and let loose. The next few hours were filled with heated looks and subtle touches between her and her pirate. The chemistry between them was undeniable, and what started as an instant attraction and flirtation quickly escalated to something hotter, sexier and oh-so-arousing.

The press of people forced her into close proximity with her hunk, not that she minded, and when she faltered on her too-high heels he caught her around the waist and brought her flush against him, searing her with the heat and strength of his body imprinting her breasts, her belly, her thighs.

That's when everything between them changed. With their hips pressed so intimately together, she could feel the hard length of him, could see the desire gleaming in his one dark blue eye. *For her.* A reckless thrill raced through her, and for what seemed like forever they stared at one another while everyone else continued to dance around them. Then his hungry, searing gaze dropped to her mouth.

Breathless with anticipation, her lips parted, and she dampened them with her tongue. That seemed to be the only invitation he needed to lower his head and kiss her... and she didn't even try to stop him. His lips were warm and soft and persuasive, seducing not only her mouth, but her senses. He deepened the kiss, his tongue tangling sensuously with hers, while one of his hands drifted over the curve of her bottom to haul her even closer. A hard thigh slid between hers, and his hips moved against hers in their own private dance—a slow, deliberate gyration that caused a pulsing, throbbing heat to settle between her legs.

She should have been mortified that she was acting so wanton in public, but she couldn't bring herself to care, not when he kissed her like a man who was dying of thirst and she was a tall, cool glass of water he couldn't get enough of. She'd never felt so desirable, had never experienced such an all-consuming sexual need.

And, oh, God, she didn't want it to end.

Too soon, he broke their potent kiss, and they were both breathing hard when he lifted his head, his gaze capturing hers in the flash of bright, colorful lights the deejay had aimed toward the dance floor. A silent, mutual acknowledgment passed between them—a bold, sexual invitation from him, and a too-easy acceptance from her.

He grabbed her hand and took charge, and she followed him as he navigated the crowd and the club, knowing that every smoldering look, every tempting touch and their deliciously drugging kiss had been building up to what they were about to do. She'd expected him to lead her down to the first floor of the club and outside somewhere, but instead he veered toward a door marked "emergency stairwell" and pulled her inside.

The door shut after them, enclosing them in a dim area that was as secluded as they were going to get for their hot, quick tryst. She had the fleeting thought that he probably did this kind of thing all the time, then immediately shoved the notion from her mind because right now, it didn't matter. Not when she was so turned on and aching for the kind of relief he could provide.

It had been a few years since she'd been with a flesh and blood man, and even then the sex had been lukewarm and nothing like the heat that was pooling in her belly and spreading like wildfire through her limbs. While she had zero experience with one-night stands, she was feeling impulsive and daring enough to let this incredibly hot guy have his way with her.

Darcie would be so proud of her for finally breaking free of the too-modest values that had been instilled in her from a young age and doing something outrageous to shake up her dull and boring love life. Having sex with a stranger in a darkened stairwell where the risk of getting caught was high was about as scandalous as she'd ever get.

With a sinful, I-can't-wait-to-have-you grin, he pressed her against the cool, concrete wall, then framed her face in his hands and locked his lips with hers and replaced every thought in her head with pure pleasure. Like the pirate he was, he plundered the depths of her mouth, using his tongue and teeth in erotic ways that made her moan and melt and primed her for so much more.

All around her, she could feel the loud pulse of the music rocking the nightclub, an encouraging beat that thrummed through her body and released something wild and wicked inside her. Determined to make the most of this onetime encounter, she slipped her hands into his unbuttoned shirt, his skin taut and blazing hot beneath the tips of her fingers. Her flattened palms boldly explored the hard, defined contours of his chest, and when her thumbs grazed his erect nipples he released a deep groan of approval that bolstered her confidence and gave her a sense of feminine empowerment.

As his mouth continued to devour hers, his hands moved, too, skimming down her neck and along her shoulders, leaving fire in the wake of his touch. His fingers caught the strap of her jungle-themed dress and tugged it down her arm to the crook of her elbow, then he pushed the cups of her strapless bra out of his way, as well. In the next instant, his mouth was on her bared breast, sucking hard, while his tongue flicked and swirled around her nipple.

Then she felt his hand between her widened legs, traveling up the inside of her thigh until he reached the elastic band of her panties. Undeterred, he slipped his fingers beneath the damp silk and stroked with such expertise and purpose that she raced quickly toward orgasm.

Pulling her breast deeper into his mouth, he increased the pressure on her clit, pushed a long finger inside her, and she plunged all ten of her fingers into his silky hair, her back arching and her breath hitching in her throat as her entire body convulsed in a shuddering orgasm.

He buried his face against her neck, the erotic brush of his breath against her skin arousing her all over again. "Jesus," he said in a voice that sounded like pure gravel. "I want you, but I don't have a condom."

Even though he'd just given her the most earth-shattering orgasm, she was still anxious to feel him inside her, and was eternally grateful that Darcie had tucked a condom into the small purse clipped to the leopard sash around her waist—in hopes that Jayne would get lucky. At the time, Jayne had humored her best friend, but as she retrieved the protection and handed it to her pirate she knew she owed Darcie a huge thank you.

The relief in her hunk's gaze spoke volumes. "You're amazing," he said, and kissed her lips again.

His compliment warmed her, spurred her, and she fumbled to open the top snap of his pants, then his zipper, to help him along. "Hurry, please."

"Impatient, too," he murmured with an amused chuckle, then groaned when she wrapped her fingers around his thick, impressive erection and gave it a squeeze.

He cursed beneath his breath and pushed her hand away so he could sheath himself. She took off her panties, unsure what to do with them until he grabbed them from her and tucked them into his pants pocket.

Suddenly, she was back against the concrete wall, his hands pushing up the skirt of her dress to her waist then hitching one of her knees over his hip. Both of his hands dropped to her backside, lifting her higher, until the broad tip of his rigid shaft found her entrance, teasing her with the promise of filling her completely.

Instinctively, she locked her ankles around his waist, and gasped in shock as he plunged inside her to the hilt. He was so large that the first thrust was almost painful, but as soon as he began to move, she softened around him and unadulterated pleasure began to vibrate through her in overwhelming waves.

She didn't think it was possible for her to have an orgasm during actual penetration, but this man and the skillful way he stroked deep inside her was proving her wrong. The slick length of him sliding in and out of her, the granite hardness of his body straining toward hers, the demanding passion of his kisses, all were designed to send her right over the edge.

Sex with him was raw and primitive, unleashing an

equally untamed side of her she never knew she possessed. She welcomed every frenzied lunge, every rough, driving thrust that pushed her higher. Fast and furious had never felt so good. Feeling as though she was spiraling out of control, she clutched at his shoulders, digging her fingers into the muscles of his back as an irrepressible tension spiraled tighter and tighter inside her.

Like a dream-fueled fantasy, her mind fogged with lust and need, and she gave herself up to what her body was chasing. As soon as she started pulsating around him, he stepped up the pace even more, then released a low, guttural growl as he came, too.

*"Wow,"* he murmured against her throat, and Jayne silently echoed his sentiment.

Long moments passed where they both tried to catch their breath, then he withdrew from her and she unlocked her ankles as he lowered her to the ground. The moment he stepped away from her, reality hit her like a slap in the face, and along with it came a heaping dose of embarrassment she could feel scorching her cheeks.

Self-conscious now, she looked away as she quickly pulled up the bodice of her jungle dress and tugged the skirt back into place. Now that their mutual itch had been scratched, she had no idea what to do or how to proceed, and he didn't seem inclined to dispel the awkwardness and uncertainty settling over her while he made some clothing adjustments of his own.

Jayne was smart enough to know that phenomenal sex did not equate to anything beyond this onetime fling, and the last thing she wanted to hear or face was a rejection from the hottest, sexiest man she'd ever been with. She refused to feel shame or regret for something that had felt so good, so before he could ruin her fantasy with some kind of lame brush-off line, she decided to leave with her pride intact while she had the chance.

"I've gotta go," she muttered, and turned toward the door and pulled it open while he was trying to zip up his pants.

The heat and noise from the nightclub hit her like a wall as she stepped back inside, and behind her she heard him call out urgently, "Wait!", but she didn't stop. Instead, she continued her escape, pushing through the crowd until the entrance was in sight. As soon as she hit the street, she hailed a cab, and once she was on her way back to her place she sent Darcie a text message telling her she had a headache and had gone home.

Now that she had time to think rationally, she couldn't believe what she'd done, how impulsive she'd been. Her behavior went against every ladylike lesson she'd ever been taught by her Aunt Millie, and she hoped she hadn't made a fool of herself with how eager and enthusiastic she'd been with him.

It was a good thing she'd never have to see him again.

# 2

*Three months later...*

"JAYNE, GWEN IS HERE to pick up her order."

Standing at the large wooden worktable in the back of her florist shop, Jayne glanced across the open area to the curtained doorway, where her best friend and store manager, Darcie, had poked her head inside.

"I'm just about done," Jayne said as she clipped the stem of a fuchsia Stargazer lily and added it to the arrangement of blue irises, white daisies, and purple statice laid out on the table. "Tell her I'll be out in less than five minutes."

"Will do," Darcie replied in a cheerful voice, before disappearing back to the store front.

Alone again, Jayne returned her attention to Gwen's bouquet. The older woman had been her first customer when she'd opened Always in Bloom four years ago. Gwen loved flowers as much as Jayne did, and every Thursday around ten in the morning she arrived to pick up whatever arrangement Jayne decided to put together for her.

Not only did Jayne appreciate Gwen's steady business, but she also enjoyed the woman's friendship. Gwen's warm and caring nature reminded her so much of her Aunt Millie, who'd passed away over five years ago after devoting her adult life to single-handedly raising Jayne.

Jayne had been orphaned at the age of seven when her parents had died in a car accident, and it had been her recently widowed Aunt Millie who'd provided her with a loving, stable home. Since Millie never had children of her own, nor had she ever remarried, Jayne had become the center of her aunt's universe.

Through the years, the two of them had bonded over the simpler things in life. Aunt Mille had taught her how to knit and sew, and made sure she learned how to cook from scratch. Instead of watching TV in the evenings, they'd read from the classics lining the bookshelves, or they'd invited Gwen over to play cribbage, rummy or mahjong. They'd spent many Sunday mornings baking pies, cakes and cookies, then took them down to the nearby retirement home for the residents to enjoy.

Growing up, Jayne had always been painfully shy and she'd been grateful for the many diversions her aunt had provided. But the hobby she'd loved the most was tending to the massive flower garden in her aunt's backyard. Together they'd planted everything from rare Victorian roses, to beautiful Ice Cream tulips, to the more vibrant orange and yellow freesia, and everything in between.

While her friends at school dated boys, or practiced cheerleading routines, and attended all the formal dances, Jayne preferred to have her hands buried in the earth's rich soil and that's where she spent most of her free time. What excited her the most was seeing the first bloom and reveal of stunning visual colors as the seeds she'd planted emerged into a breath taking botanical display.

She'd gone on to major in horticulture, and when her aunt died and left her with a sizeable inheritance, she'd decided to honor the woman who raised her by opening her own flower shop. Thus, Always in Bloom had been born, and the boutique had quickly grown into a thriving business that had consumed most of Jayne's time, but it was a labor of love she didn't mind.

Jayne finished off Gwen's bouquet with a sprinkling of baby's breath, then wrapped up the flowers in a cellophane sleeve and added a pretty violet ribbon bow. She carried the arrangement out to the front, where Darcie was ringing up a potted plant for another customer, and Gwen was sitting at the table Jayne had set up as a place for people to wait for their order.

Wearing black slacks and a patterned silk blouse accented with a string of pearls around her neck, the older woman looked well put together, as always. Her dyed-brown hair had been recently colored and styled, her make-up was immaculately applied and made her look much younger than her actual age of sixty-eight, and she sat in her chair looking every inch a lady who was used to the finer things in life.

"Here you go, Gwen." Jayne greeted her friend with a smile. "I received some beautiful Stargazer lilies this morning and couldn't resist using them in your bouquet. What do you think?"

"They're absolutely beautiful," Gwen said, her pale blue eyes sparkling with delight as Jayne placed the flowers on the table in front of her. "Then again, you've yet to disappoint me with your selections. That's why I gave you free rein. It's always a fun surprise to see what you put together for me."

"Good, I'm glad."

Gwen looked around the shop just as the woman who'd bought the potted plant left the store, then glanced back at Jayne. "Do you have a few minutes to talk?"

"Sure." She had nothing pressing to do, so she sat down in the chair across from Gwen, her curiosity piqued.

Gwen folded her hands on the table, her expression turning serious. "Do you realize that my wedding to Patrick is already next weekend?"

"Your wedding is on Valentine's Day, which is hard to forget," Jayne replied with amusement. Gwen was heading into her fifth marriage, to a man she claimed was "the love of her life", and she was doing it up big for the ceremony and reception. "Not only is it the most romantic day of the year, but I'm making all your flower bouquets and arrangements, so I know exactly how many days it is until you tie the knot."

Jayne suddenly wondered if there was a more pressing reason for Gwen to have brought up the short time frame of her upcoming nuptials. "Is everything okay with you and Patrick?"

"Everything is perfectly wonderful with Patrick. He is, after all, the man of my dreams." Gwen sighed like only a woman in love could. "Actually, I'm more concerned about *you*."

Startled and a little confused, Jayne pressed a hand to her chest. "You're worried about *me?* Why?"

"Because I received your RSVP card for the wedding in the mail the other day, and you only responded for a party of *one*."

Jayne didn't see why that was a cause for concern. "Yes. Just me."

"It's Valentine's Day, sweetie," Gwen said, her eyes as soft and caring as her voice. "You can't come to the wedding without a date. Even Darcie has a boyfriend to bring."

"Yes, I do," Darcie piped in enthusiastically from where

she was watering a nearby gardenia plant. "And, as you both know, he's absolutely *dreamy*."

Darcie released an uncharacteristically besotted sigh to equal the one Gwen had just exhaled, and Jayne couldn't help but roll her eyes at all the lovey-dovey vibes the two women were putting off. Darcie's latest boyfriend, Josh, was the vampire she'd met at the Halloween party at the nightclub three months ago, and what had begun as a heated physical attraction between the two had gradually given way to a deeper interest, and just recently, love.

Jayne was truly happy for her best friend, who deserved a good man in her life, which Josh definitely was in spades. But sometimes, knowing that Darcie's relationship with Josh had begun on the night they met, after what Darcie referred to as the most orgasmic sex she'd ever had with a guy, Jayne was often left pondering a slew of "what-if" scenarios with her pirate. The most prominent one being, what if she hadn't let old securities get the best of her and had stayed that night, instead of bolted?

Unfortunately, and regretfully, she'd never know the answer to that question.

Having been raised by her reserved aunt and surrounded by Millie's older generation of friends, she'd always been swayed towards dating older, more stable men that her aunt approved of. The few relationships she'd been involved in had been comfortable, and while she and those men had been intellectually compatible, sexually she'd always felt as though something important was missing.

With her pirate, she'd had a taste of lust and passion and now knew exactly what had been lacking in her previous relationships—an undeniable physical attraction and burning desire. A part of her regretted that she hadn't been bold and confident enough to stick around and see if there could be something more between her and her pirate than a quick, heated encounter in a darkened stairwell.

Dressed as Jungle Jane in a place where no one knew her identity, she'd been able to let a more provocative persona take over and see where it took her. Their encounter had stemmed from the forbidden, and the illusion that she was this wild and wanton woman, but in her real everyday life, she was far from spontaneous or impulsive—and she was crazy to think she could have a relationship or future with a man as sexy and exciting as her pirate.

Yet knowing all that, it didn't stop her from laying in bed at night, her body tingling as she conjured up that night in her mind and recalled her pirate's kisses, his seductive caresses, and how he'd literally rocked her world as he pumped deep inside her, waiting for her to climax before he took his own pleasure. Her pirate had definitely set the bar high for the next man she slept with, and she often wondered if anyone would ever be able to live up to the standards he'd set for her.

"Earth to Jayne," Darcie said, her singsong voice jolting Jayne back to the present. "Are you still with us?"

Realizing her thoughts had drifted off to a place better left in the past, she shifted in her seat and smoothed a hand down her gauzy skirt, trying to quickly recall what they'd been discussing before she'd taken a trip down memory lane. Oh, yeah, Gwen was worried because Jayne was attending her wedding solo and didn't have a man in her life to celebrate Valentine's Day.

"It's not a big deal that I don't have a date. Really," Jayne insisted. She'd spent many Valentine's Days by herself, and was grateful that as a florist it was the busiest week, and day, of the year for her, so she never had much time to think about the fact that she didn't have a special someone in her life.

"I happen to think differently," Gwen said with a regal-like wave of her hand. The morning sun streaming through the window glinted off the massive diamond on her left hand, nearly blinding Jayne from the brilliant shine of her engagement ring. "And it just so happens that I have the perfect man in mind for you."

Jayne managed, just barely, to suppress a groan. "Another blind date?"

Darcie, who was standing behind Gwen plucking wilted blooms from a hanging basket of deep purple wisteria, smirked at Jayne. She knew all the disastrous details of Gwen's other attempts to set Jayne up, and she dreaded the thought of having to go through that torture again.

But Gwen loved to play matchmaker whenever she could, which Jayne found amusing considering Gwen had been married and divorced four times, and was getting ready to head down the aisle for the fifth.

In that regard, when it came to love and marriage, Gwen and Jayne's aunt couldn't have been more opposite in their views. Millie had never remarried because she believed there was only one love of your life, and she'd always disapproved of her friend's many relationships and unions. Jayne's aunt had always considered Gwen to be a little wanton and shameless when it came to men, and never hesitated to use Gwen as an example of the kind of behavior she refused to allow her young niece to emulate.

But secretly, Jayne had always admired Gwen's zest for passion and love and life, and her ability to go after what she wanted and not worry about what others felt or thought.

The older woman reached across the table and patted Jayne's hand affectionately, bringing her attention back to the present. "I know I might have missed the mark a tad last time, but I have a really good feeling about this man."

Truthfully, Gwen had missed the mark by a *mile* when she'd arranged a blind date between her accountant's son and Jayne. Sure, the guy had been good looking, but he'd also been way too cocky and arrogant when it came to his appeal to the opposite sex. They'd had absolutely nothing in common, and not only had he dominated most of the conversation for the evening—when he wasn't texting or talking on his cell phone—he'd left her footing the bill for dinner after his credit card had been declined. Then he'd had the audacity to kiss her, tongue and all.

Ugh. It was an experience she had no desire to repeat.

"Brian's incredibly handsome, and quite the gentleman which is hard to find these days," Gwen went on in her attempt to sway her. "And he's very successful and owns his own practice. He's quite the catch."

A smile lifted the corner of Jayne's mouth. "If he's such a catch, then why isn't he already taken?"

Gwen shrugged, as if the answer was a no-brainer. "Because he obviously hasn't found 'the one' yet."

Jayne was certain the reason why this Brian guy was still single wasn't that simple or sentimental, just as she was certain that she wasn't the woman of his dreams. "How do you know him?"

"He's Bella's veterinarian," Gwen said of the cute little Maltese she'd adopted a few years ago.

A doctor. She admitted to being impressed, but she just couldn't bring herself to go through another blind date of Gwen's choosing, no matter how good her intentions might be.

"I appreciate the thought, but I'm really not interested," she said, doing her best to gently turn her down.

Gwen wasn't having any of it. "How can you say you're not interested when you haven't even met him yet? I've known him for over two years now, and he's such a nice, polite young man. When I saw that he didn't have a date for my wedding either, I knew it was fate that I set the two of you up."

Jayne had to suppress the urge to laugh at the older woman's reasoning, but as much as she didn't want to agree to the date, she didn't want to offend Gwen, either. "Did you ever think that maybe he prefers to attend the wedding by himself, like I do?"

Gwen blinked much too innocently. "If that was the case, then why did he already agree to a blind date with you?"

Surprise rippled through Jayne. "He *did?*"

"Without hesitation," Gwen said, then pulled her wallet from her purse and withdrew a business card. "In fact, he gave me his personal cell phone number and he's waiting for you to call him to let him know when you're free for dinner."

It all sounded much too desperate to Jayne, like maybe the guy couldn't get a date on his own and was eager to take whatever he could get. Reluctantly, she took the card from Gwen, and read the imprinted name on it: Brian Reeves, DVM. She even recognized the name of his animal hospital, Advanced Pet Care, which was located a few miles away from Always in Bloom.

As if sensing Jayne was still trying to think up an excuse to avoid the blind date, Gwen tried a guilt tactic. "You wouldn't want to disappoint him, now would you?"

Jayne was very tempted to do just that.

"Give it up, Jayne," Darcie said as she straightened a rack of greeting cards and continued her eavesdropping. "Besides, it's one date, not a lifetime commitment."

"Exactly," Gwen chimed in, her gaze still optimistic.

Honestly, it wasn't the overly anxious vet Jayne was worried about disappointing, but Gwen. She really did adore her, and knew the older woman's heart was in the right place in wanting Jayne to find a man she could spend the rest of her life with. But after the last blind date Gwen had set her up on, Jayne didn't have a whole lot of hope that this one would end up much better.

Still, she knew she couldn't say no to a woman who'd been so good to her the past couple of years. "Fine, I'll go," she said, and the elation on Gwen's face made her agreement almost worth it.

She'd go to dinner with Brian Reeves, spend a few hours in his company, fulfill her end of the blind-date bargain, and at the end of the night pull the "let's be friends" card, which was the best way to avoid any hard feelings.

Friendship was good, especially since she'd have to see him again at Gwen's wedding.

# 3

BRIAN ARRIVED AT the oceanfront restaurant where he and his blind date had agreed to meet, thirty minutes earlier than the reservation he'd made for dinner. He checked in with the hostess to make sure that they'd have a table near the windows overlooking the water, then let the young girl know he'd be over at the bar until his date arrived.

The seafood restaurant was one of San Diego's most popular, and even though it was a Thursday evening, the place was quickly filling up. Since he wanted the advantage of seeing her first, Brian took a seat at the bar that gave him a direct view of the hostess stand, then ordered a Jack and coke to nurse while he waited.

As soon as the bartender delivered his drink, he took a sip, still unable to believe he'd let Gwen rope him into going on a blind date. He'd never had a problem getting a date on his own, and preferred to do so. But when Gwen had come into his office a week ago to get her Maltese updated on her shots, she'd caught him in a semi-compromising situation with another woman who'd spent the past few weeks attempting to seduce him, and was using a multitude of fake excuses about her dog's health to see him.

Shelly wasn't his type, not by a long shot. She had big

bleached blond hair, wore skin-tight pants with even tighter T-shirts that were so low-cut they revealed nearly half of her large, surgically enhanced breasts. Not only did he like his women all natural, with real curves and softer bodies, but he also liked them to possess a certain level of class and sophistication. Especially in public.

Numerous times, he'd gently turned Shelly down, but she clearly believed he was just playing hard to get and it was only a matter of time before he caved. He'd remained polite and professional, even as he'd grown increasingly annoyed over the fact that she was using her Jack Russell to get to him.

But her last visit to the pet clinic had been the clincher. Just when she thought the two of them were alone in the reception area, as soon as he delivered the news that the latest test results on her dog were negative and he saw no reason for Shelly to bring the Jack Russell in again, she'd plastered herself against him like an octopus in heat. She wound her arms tight around his neck, entwined one of her legs around his, and planted her lips to his in an aggressive, open-mouthed kiss.

Her attack had taken him completely off guard, and before he could diffuse the situation, Gwen had walked in on the two of them, her eyes wide with shock. He had to admit the scenario looked bad. Really bad. And it was more than awkward, to say the least, getting caught in such an embarrassing position by someone he liked and respected as much as Gwen.

It had taken a good amount of effort to disengage Shelly, but at that moment he knew what he had to do. He'd informed her that he could no longer treat her dog, and gave her the business card of another vet in town. She'd left in a huff, but at least he'd finally made his point that he wasn't interested.

Once Shelly was gone and he'd escorted Gwen and her Maltese, Bella, into a private exam room, the older woman hadn't wasted any time in chastising him for his behavior— even though it hadn't been his fault—like his own mother would have. If that hadn't been exasperating enough, she'd then insisted that she was going to find a *nice* girl for him because she didn't want him to end up with a hussy like Shelly. Better yet, Gwen knew a sweet woman who didn't have a date for the wedding either, and she was absolutely certain they would hit it off. And how great would it be that the two of them could attend the ceremony as a couple, instead of being alone and single on Valentine's Day?

The woman had been like a dog with a bone who wouldn't let go. While checking Bella's ears then listening to her heartbeat, he'd tried to gracefully bow out of the blind date by telling Gwen it just wasn't his thing, but she wasn't easily deterred. Instead, she'd enlightened him to the fact that the woman, Jayne, had already agreed to the date—which seemed a bit desperate to him—and he knew he'd look like a jerk if he refused.

So, reluctantly, he'd said yes. A day later Jayne had called his cell phone, and they'd agreed to a weeknight date the following Wednesday—something easy and casual since both of them had to work the next day. The arrangement was more than fine with Brian, and gave them both the opportunity to call it an early evening if they weren't the perfect match Gwen believed them to be.

Twenty minutes after first sitting at the bar, Brian spotted a woman walking through the doors to the restaurant, her black and purple outfit matching the color description Jayne had given him over the phone. She stood in line to check in with the hostess, giving him a few extra moments to finish his drink and observe her from a distance before they met face to face.

At least Gwen hadn't lied when she said that Jayne was pretty. Her silky, honey blonde hair was cut into a stylish, layered, shoulder length bob, and she seemed to be wearing minimal make-up—just enough to enhance her eyes, and some shimmery gloss on her lips. She was dressed more conservatively than the women he normally dated, in a purple blouse, a loose, flowing, black skirt and a pair of low-heeled shoes. There was nothing overtly flashy about her—she was the antithesis of Shelly in every way—and he found her entire appearance and ladylike demeanor a refreshing change.

Pleasantly surprised by his date, Brian slid off his barstool and made his way back to the front of the restaurant just as she reached the hostess stand. After a brief exchange, the hostess glanced back toward the bar and pointed at him. Jayne pasted on a smile and stepped toward him, and as he neared and got a closer look at her face, an overwhelming sense of familiarity washed over him.

Images of a woman in a sexy, one-shouldered, leopard print dress flashed through his mind, taking him back to that provocative night with her at the club. He'd seen up close and personal how those dark brown eyes of hers could turn hazy with desire, had tasted those lush lips and reveled in her uninhibited response to his touch. He also knew that the body beneath the simple outfit she wore now was soft and curvy, and fit his like a dream.

Three months might have passed, but he hadn't forgotten that night. Or her. She'd left an indelible imprint on his mind, and too often he'd wondered how things would have progressed between the two of them if only she'd stayed, instead of bolting while he still had his pants down.

But he'd just been given a second chance thanks to Gwen, and he planned to take full advantage of his lucky break.

Grinning, he stopped in front of her and held out his hand in greeting. "I'm Brian Reeves. You must be Jayne." He deliberately used the same line on her that he had when he'd first met her at the nightclub. Little did he know then that his Jungle Jane really *was* Jayne.

"I *am* Jayne," she replied, and as she slipped her hand into his to shake and looked into his eyes, the polite smile on her lips faltered.

He knew the precise second recognition hit her. Her eyes grew wide, her lips parted in shock, and a panicked look swept across her features. With her soft, slender hand enclosed in his, he felt her jerk back in startled surprise, but he didn't let go.

"Oh, my God," she said in a strangled voice. "You're the pirate."

"That would be me." He gentled his hold, but still didn't release her. Now that he'd found her again, he wasn't letting her go so easily. "So, we meet again."

Seemingly still in shock, she shook her head, the silky sway of her hair framing her delicate features. "This has to be some kind of mistake."

"A coincidence, definitely," he admitted with a smile. "But it's no mistake. You and I were set up with the best of intentions by Gwen, and I owe her big-time. I've spent the past three months wondering what I did to make you run off before we could even exchange names. I thought we had a strong connection." Holding her gaze, he rubbed his thumb over the pulse in her wrist and felt her shiver from his caress. Physical proof that there was still a level of heated awareness simmering between them.

"We only knew each other for a few hours," she said, her rationale thin and flimsy. "Hardly enough time to make any kind of connection."

"I'm going to have to disagree," he murmured, and knew

there was one thing she wouldn't be able to deny, no matter how hard she tried. He dipped his head toward hers, keeping his voice low so only she could hear. "Sexually, we connected quite well. Unless you were faking those orgasms?"

Her face flushed a bright shade of red, her embarrassment real enough to indicate that she wasn't the kind of woman who had a lot of experience with one-night stands. "I really can't do this with you," she said, the dismay in her voice matching the unsettled emotions in her eyes.

If he was an egotistical man, she would have crushed his male pride by now. But he was a confident and patient guy, one who believed that good things came to those who waited. A sexual attraction might have initially brought them together, but he'd dated enough women to know that there was a lot more substance to Jayne. Like that underlying vulnerability that intrigued and drew him, and a refreshing honesty he appreciated.

It was also difficult not to be aware of the obvious differences between Jungle Jane and this Jayne. Jungle Jane had been seductive and tempting. This Jayne was modest and far more self-conscious. It was an interesting contradiction. Ultimately, his gut told him that Jayne Young was a special and unique woman with a hidden sensuality just waiting for the right man to tap into. He'd had a taste of that wild eroticism, and suspected there was a whole lot more where that came from.

She was definitely a woman worth pursuing, for a variety of reasons, but getting her to agree was going to be another matter.

"Your window table is ready," the hostess said, interrupting their conversation as she came up to them with menus in hand.

"Come on, Jayne," he urged, and gave the hand he was

still holding a gentle, encouraging squeeze. "We're both already here. It's just dinner and I promise to be on my best behavior."

He watched her struggle with some inner conflict he didn't understand, then she released a deep breath and straightened her shoulders—which served to tighten her blouse across her soft, full breasts. "Okay. Let's do it."

*Let's do it*. He almost teased her over the double entendre, but didn't want to risk losing the ground he'd gained by embarrassing her again. The hostess walked into the dining area, and with a hand pressed to Jayne's lower back, Brian escorted her in the same direction, then held out a chair for her to sit facing the ocean view before taking a seat right next to her.

With Jayne's input on her preference of wine, he ordered a bottle of Pinot Noir. They were both quiet for a few moments as they perused the menu and decided what they wanted for dinner. Their waitress came back with the wine, poured them each a glass, and took their order. Once she was gone and they were alone again, Brian turned his attention to Jayne, who was smoothing her cloth napkin on her lap.

"Can I ask you something, Jayne?" he asked, keeping his voice light and neutral.

Despite his casual tone, a flicker of wariness crept into her gaze. "Sure," she said, not sounding certain at all.

He took a drink of his wine, and watched her do the same. "Why did you run out on me that night at the club?"

She set her glass back down, averted her gaze, and began fiddling with her fork. "Because I didn't want you to think that I'm *that* kind of girl."

He placed a hand over hers to stop her nervous fidgeting, and to force her to look back at him. In his estimation, the kind of girl she'd been with him, so sweet and hot and giving, wasn't a bad thing. But for some reason, she thought differently and he wanted to know why.

"What kind of girl is that?" he asked, genuinely curious to know her thoughts.

"You know…" Flustered once again, she pulled her hand from beneath his and waved it in the air between them, as if grasping for the right words to describe her behavior that night.

He found them for her. "Sexy? Desirable? Irresistible?" he asked, supplying all the adjectives that exemplified the woman he'd met three months ago. The woman he knew she still was despite her protective outer layers and demure demeanor that made her appear too prim and proper.

"I'm not *promiscuous*," she said, using a description that never would have crossed his mind had she not said it. "I don't go around sleeping with men on a whim. I'm sure you're used to that kind of thing with women, but for me, it just…happened."

He believed her, and wanted her to know that it wasn't a normal occurrence for him, as well. "I don't go around having sex with women I just met, either," he stated. "And just for the record, I'm very discriminate about who I have sex with. Like you, what we did that night at the club just happened. I didn't plan it."

She lifted a dubious brow, and he laughed at her skepticism.

"You don't believe me?" he asked.

She shrugged. "Your actions that night showed otherwise, not that I'm complaining."

It was a double-standard statement, and he didn't hesitate to point that out to her, grinning while he did so. "So did *your* actions, not that *I'm* complaining."

She blinked at him, and for a moment he thought she

was going to take offense. Then, unexpectedly, the lightest, sweetest laughter escaped her, the sound disintegrating the fine line of tension between them and immediately lightening the mood.

"Fine," she said on a sigh, even as a smile teased the corner of her mouth. "It just happened. For the both of us."

"And it was *amazing*," he added, wanting her to know exactly how he felt about her, and that night.

"Yeah, it was," she agreed softly.

He wanted so much to lean in and kiss her at that moment, to give her a physical reminder of what fantastic chemistry they had together. But before he could execute the move the waitress arrived with their dinner. She placed a dish of seared scallops and rice pilaf in front of Jayne, and grilled salmon and fingerling potatoes for him.

Now that they were on the same page regarding their attraction, he decided to take their discussion in a different, more personal direction in an attempt to get to know her better.

"Gwen tells me you're a florist, and you own Always in Bloom in town," he said as he speared his fork into a bite of salmon. "Tell me about that."

She didn't hesitate to talk about her business, giving credence to the fact that he'd chosen the right topic to get her to open up. She talked about her shop, her love of gardening and flowers, and how her Aunt Millie, the woman who'd raised her, was responsible for instilling a deep appreciation for nature and anything that blossomed from the earth's soil. She was animated and naturally endearing, and he was fascinated to see this whole different side to Jayne that completed the woman she was.

As they enjoyed their dinner and wine, he encouraged her to talk with questions of his own, and learned about the car accident that had claimed her parents' lives, and what her childhood had been like with her Aunt Millie. She'd had a stable, loving upbringing, but as she chatted about her aunt it became clear to Brian that some of Jayne's more modest and reserved traits had been due to her aunt's influence.

They talked about music, movies and books, and had a lot more in common than either of them would have thought. She seemed surprised to discover that some of the classics she'd read growing up, like *Call of The Wild* and *Treasure Island*, were some of his favorites, too. They both enjoyed jazz music, and while he would have pegged her for a romantic comedy kind of girl when it came to movies, she admitted to being a Hitchcock fan and loved thrillers as much as he did.

She asked about his family, and he told her about his parents, who'd been married for over thirty-five years and were still madly in love. He regaled her with amusing tales about growing up with his two older sisters that made her laugh, and how he was a total nerd in high school, which she said she found hard to believe.

"What made you decide to become a veterinarian?" she asked, right before she took a bite of one of her scallops.

"My father was a veterinarian," he replied as he refilled both their wine glasses. "As a kid, I spent my weekends at his clinic, cleaning cages and assisting him when he needed the extra help. I've always loved animals, so it was an easy, natural transition to become a vet like my dad. We worked together for a few years after I got my license, and when he had a heart attack and decided to retire, I took over the business for him."

"Sounds like we're both nurturers," she said with a smile. "Me with my plants and flowers, and you with animals."

"I guess so." He watched as she took a long sip of her

Pinot Noir, intrigued more than ever by everything he'd learned about her tonight.

By the end of their meal she'd relaxed and loosened up. She was smiling, her brown eyes were bright, and her expression was happy. He ordered a chocolate truffle cake for them to share, and she was now so comfortable with him that when it arrived she took her fork and went in for the first bite, which was followed by a deep, throaty moan of appreciation as she tasted the rich, decadent dessert.

Her enthusiasm made him chuckle. The rapturous look on her face made him hard. "I take it you like the cake?"

As if realizing how eager she'd been, she ducked her head and one of those engaging blushes swept across her cheeks. "God, I'm shameless," she murmured. "I love chocolate, and I love cake. Put the two of them together and I can't resist."

"Go for it." He pushed the plate closer to her. "It's nice to see a woman who isn't afraid to appreciate a good dessert."

She tipped her head. "Aren't you going to help me eat it?"

"I'll have a bite or two, but I'd much rather watch you enjoy it."

She didn't argue, and as a result she provided him with enough fuel for a dozen different fantasies, arousing him with the sensual roll of her eyes, a soft groan of pleasure as she swallowed a bite, and the slow glide of her tongue across her bottom lip as she licked away a smear of chocolate. He knew her seductive moves were uncalculated, which made it all the more of a turn on. He shifted in his chair to relieve the pressure straining against his zipper, and wondered if she realized the effect she had on him.

Probably not, but he intended to enlighten her before their date was over.

After eating the last morsel, she put her fork down and sighed contentedly. "That was *amazing.*"

Her comment was the same one he'd made about their hot night together at the club. He took in the glow on her face, and all he could think about was sex. With her. Again. "Yeah, it was."

His comment wasn't lost on her, and served to elevate the awareness that had been building between them all evening long.

He paid the check, and since they'd driven separate cars, he walked Jayne to hers. With every step they took toward her vehicle, she grew quiet and he suspected that a new batch of nerves was getting the best of her. When she turned toward him with her hand outstretched and a polite "Thank you for dinner," falling from her lips, he knew he was going to have to be a little more creative in order to make Jayne see that there was something worth exploring between them. He wasn't about to lose all the ground he'd just gained with her with a platonic handshake.

Slipping his hand in hers, he used it as an anchor to slowly pull her closer. "I'd rather have a kiss."

"I...I think we should just remain friends."

The longing in her golden brown gaze contradicted her too-formal request. He wasn't sure why she was so hesitant, but he was more than prepared to cajole her to his way of thinking.

Another gentle tug, and she was in his arms, her body pressed against his. When she didn't resist, he looped her arms around his neck, placed one of his flattened palms at the base of her spine, and threaded the fingers of his other hand through her softer-than-silk hair until he held her securely in his embrace.

Her breathing deepened, and her lips parted in anticipation. It seemed that all she needed was a little guidance, and he was more than happy to provide it.

"Yeah, we can be friends, too," he murmured, and set out to show her that while friendship was a good, strong foundation when it came to any relationship, the kind of hot physical chemistry they had together was an added bonus for both of them to enjoy.

The initial touch of their lips was soft and sweet, and when his mouth nudged hers in an encouraging gesture, she released a moan of surrender and made the first move to deepen the kiss, which he welcomed. She pressed closer, crushing her breasts against his chest as her fingers fisted in his hair. Clinging to him, she drew his tongue into her mouth, the slick heat and firm pressure of her lips on his spiraling straight to his groin in a rush of desire.

The guttural groan that erupted from his chest was an instinctive response to her seduction, primitive and purely male, and unlike anything he'd ever felt before. In a haze of lust, he realized this is what he'd waited three, long months for, and why no other woman since then had tempted him the way Jayne did.

She was, quite possibly, the one he'd been waiting for.

Every little thing he discovered about Jayne only made him like her more. They shared a lot of the same family values, and she was genuine, unpretentious and real. An intelligent, successful business woman who was passionate about what she did in life.

At this moment, he knew that passion of hers ran much deeper. She might be a lady in public, but in private...oh, Lord, he knew she had the ability to bring him to his knees, in the very best way.

Now that she'd given him all the ammunition he needed to coax her into giving the two of them a chance, he lifted his head and stared into her dark, hazy eyes. "You want me," he said, and grinned, knowing she'd be hard pressed to deny his statement after the hungry way she'd just kissed him.

She licked her damp bottom lip, as if tasting him again. "What woman wouldn't want you?"

Her opinion was the only one that mattered to him. "I like you, Jayne. A lot," he said as he stroked his hand up and down her back, wishing she was naked instead of fully clothed so he could feel her smooth skin beneath his palms. "And if it isn't already obvious, I want you, too."

She shook her head, a slight frown marring her brows. "No, you want the woman you met at the nightclub."

When she tried to pull away, he tightened his hold on her, taken aback by her comment and wanting clarification. "What do you mean?"

A soft sigh unraveled out of her. Her arms slid from around his neck, and her fingers played with the collar of his shirt—a sign he now recognized as a nervous gesture. "I'm talking about the daring, adventurous woman who had sex with you in a stairwell. But that was a onetime thing and isn't who I am. I'm actually quite ordinary."

She'd averted her gaze, and he tipped her chin back up so he could look into her eyes. "Trust me, sweetheart. You're far from ordinary." She fascinated him on all levels.

He'd also seen that daring, exciting, adventurous woman three months ago and knew she existed, but Jayne obviously didn't believe in her own sensuality. But now that she'd given him a glimpse of her upbringing with her staid, old-fashioned aunt, he had a better understanding of why she was so uncertain of her ability to seduce a man.

When she didn't respond, he decided to take on a different tactic, one that would be difficult for her to refuse and would give him more time with her without her feeling intimidated. She might be able to turn him down easily, but he had a feeling that for Gwen, she'd be more accommodating.

"Tell you what. Gwen set the two of us up because she thought we were a good match. I happen to agree." He feathered his thumb along her jaw line, then down the side of her neck until he felt her shiver from his caress. "She told me you were also invited to her rehearsal dinner Friday night, and she asked me to be there, too. So, let's make her happy and go as a couple to the dinner, and the wedding. We can enjoy each other's company for the next few days, then re-evaluate our relationship and where it might be headed after this weekend. What do you say?"

She worried on her bottom lip, and he could see the debate she was warring within herself. Should she, or shouldn't she? But somewhere along the way, their attraction won out over any doubts she might have harbored.

"I say...*yes*."

# 4

*She'd said yes.*

Jayne lay in bed later that night, her mind replaying her response to Brian's proposition to spend the next few days together to make Gwen happy on her wedding day. While she'd originally agreed because she didn't want to let Gwen down, now, all alone, Jayne was forced to admit her reasons for saying yes to Brian went much deeper than pleasing her friend.

Jayne longed to please herself for a change, and if she was honest, she *wanted* to spend more time with Brian, even if it was only a few more days. Because unlike any other guy she'd ever dated, the undeniable attraction between them was hot and exciting, and for once in her life she wanted to embrace the erotic sensations he inspired and go with it.

Feeling sexy and desirable was all so new and different for her, and while she didn't have a whole lot of experience when it came to sexually confident men like Brian, she knew he was capable of giving her the greatest pleasure imaginable.

Unbidden, vivid images of the wicked things he'd done to her in that stairwell three months ago washed through

Jayne's mind, and her body responded to those provocative recollections. Brian's mouth ravishing hers. His clever tongue finessing her nipple before he sucked the tip deep and hard. Long fingers stroking her sex and bringing her to a shattering climax that made every orgasm that had come before pale in comparison.

And the entire time she'd responded so shamelessly—her hands tangling desperately in his hair, her body arching wantonly for more, her legs widening for his touch. Then she'd brazenly reached between them to take his thick shaft in her hand, shocking even herself with her bold move. But then he'd groaned his approval and desire had been quick to take over, and she'd instinctively stroked and caressed all that masculine heat and hardness, so eager to feel him thrusting deep inside her body.

And when he'd finally filled her up, she'd gone wild with a need so intense it was as if she couldn't get enough of him. For someone with little experience with such all-consuming ecstasy, the emotion had been frightening and overwhelming, and the wanton woman she'd become in that moment had been enough to make her bolt in the aftermath.

Closing her eyes, she shifted restlessly on her cool sheets as her trip down memory lane caused a rush of warmth to settle between her thighs, making her wish that Brian was with her now to ease the ache spreading through her. There was no doubt that he'd brought out a passionate side to her that she never knew existed, just as there was no denying that she'd liked how daring she'd felt with him. And for a few more days, she wanted to be the kind of bold and spontaneous woman who could keep a man like Brian satisfied.

She had nothing to lose, and everything, including immense pleasure, to gain.

THE NEXT MORNING at ten o'clock, Gwen arrived to pick up her weekly Thursday floral arrangement. As Jayne carried out a wrapped bouquet of Carnelian Mokara Orchids, the first thing she saw was Gwen's bright and eager expression. While Jayne would have liked to think the other woman's anticipation was due to the vibrant orange hue of the exotic flowers she'd chosen to put together, Jayne knew Gwen well enough to know she was more anxious to hear how her matchmaking skills had fared.

"Those orchids are gorgeous, Jayne," Gwen said, her polite compliment quickly giving way to the curiosity gleaming in her eyes. "So, how was your date with Brian last night? Did the two of you hit it off like I thought you would? Isn't he just the most handsome man you've ever met? And such a gentleman, too."

Gwen didn't have to sell Jayne on Brian's attributes. Jayne was already infatuated with the man, in a big way. "It was a very nice date."

"Just *nice?*" Gwen wrinkled her nose in disappointment. Obviously, she was hoping for the juicier results of their evening together.

While Jayne wasn't about to give Gwen a detailed report of her previous one-night stand with Brian, or their too-arousing kiss last night, she provided just enough to let the other woman believe she'd succeeded with this latest match of hers. "We clicked quite well, and I like him very much," she replied truthfully.

*"And?"* Gwen leaned across the counter, her gaze expectant as she waited to hear how the date had concluded.

Jayne smiled and gave her what she was angling for. A positive ending to last night's date. "And we'll be going to the rehearsal dinner together tomorrow night, and the wedding, too."

"I'm so thrilled." Gwen pressed a hand to her heart and

released a delightful sigh. "I just knew the two of you would make a perfect match."

Jayne wasn't so sure that she and Brian were perfect for one another, but the two of them had agreed to spend the next few days together to make Gwen happy on her wedding day. Being with Brian over the weekend certainly wasn't going to be a hardship considering how gorgeous and charming the man was, but everything about Brian made her want *more*.

More of him. More easygoing dates like they'd shared last night, where they'd connected on more than just a physical level and had enjoyed one another's company.

And, Lord help her, she wanted to experience more hot, spontaneous, unreserved sex like they'd had three months ago in a darkened stairwell.

As she charged the bouquet of orchids to Gwen's account, a flush of heat suffused her cheeks. When had her thoughts become so shameless? The answer came easily—the night she'd met her exciting, sexy pirate and he'd shown her just how good—no, how *phenomenal*—sex could actually be.

Since she was spending the weekend with Brian, she wanted one more night like the one at the club. He'd already made it clear that he wanted her, but she needed to give him the right signals to proceed, and she didn't know how.

Being raised by her sweet but old-fashioned Aunt Millie, Jayne had been instilled with a good-girl mentality from a very early age, and it wasn't an easy habit to break. But Darcie excelled in the art of flirtation and knew how to tempt and tease a man with the promise of pleasure, and Jayne hoped her friend could help her tap into her inner bad girl and give her the tips she needed to seduce Brian one last time.

That was Jayne's plan, anyway. It remained to be seen if she'd be successful.

"I can't wait to see the two of you tomorrow night." Gwen grinned, openly satisfied that her plan had worked like a charm. "Now I'm off to pick up my wedding dress."

Gwen gave Jayne a big hug, then gathered up her orchids and left the shop.

The rest of the day passed quickly for Jayne. Orders for Valentine's Day continued to pour in, and the extra help that she'd hired for the holiday was busy in the back of the shop putting together the various bouquets and arrangements for Valentine's, with Darcie supervising the process. Jayne worked on the delivery schedule, and double-checked floral displays as they were completed, then started on the arrangements for Gwen's wedding, which Jayne planned on delivering personally before the ceremony started since she'd be there, anyway.

Knowing she was going to be putting in a later night than usual so she could take tomorrow evening off for the rehearsal dinner, Jayne encouraged Darcie to take a late lunch with her at a nearby café. After their Cobb salads were delivered, Jayne gathered the courage to tell her friend about her plan to seduce Brian—and how she desperately needed Darcie's help to make sure she didn't fumble in her attempts to entice him.

An hour later, Jayne was armed with an arsenal of tantalizing tricks guaranteed to get Brian hot and bothered before the main event. According to Darcie, men were physical and visual creatures, and it was all about the slow build up of sexual tension, and arousing a man's five senses along the way. Her advice included Jayne wearing a light spray of perfume in strategic places that would tempt his sense of smell, and making sure whatever outfit she wore gave Brian plenty of skin, and cleavage, to look at to increase his awareness of her. Whisper intimate things in his ear, and don't forget the power of a subtle caress to raise the level of heat and attraction between them.

It all seemed simple enough…for someone who had experience. For Jayne, she knew she was going to have to stretch beyond her own personal comfort zone and ignore her more modest sensibilities in order to become that bold and brazen woman. If the pay-off was anything like that night at the club with Brian, she was willing to give Darcie's suggestions a try.

After lunch, Darcie insisted on accompanying Jayne on a quick shopping spree at the trendy boutique next to the café to find a new dress for her to wear—one that would make Brian's jaw drop when he picked her up for the rehearsal dinner. After giving a big thumbs down to Jayne's first three outfit choices, Darcie selected a sexy pink and black wrap around dress from a rack, declaring it the perfect dress to tease a man's imagination. Jayne also bought a new bra and panty set, and a pair of black heels that were higher and racier than anything she already owned.

Multiple bags in hand, they headed back to Always in Bloom and worked until after nine that evening. As soon as Jayne got home, she took a hot shower, put on a pair of cotton pajamas, and got into bed. She was too keyed-up to go right to sleep, so she reached for the novel on her nightstand and decided to read until she was sleepy.

At ten-fifteen, her cell phone rang. No one ever called her that late. When she checked to see who was calling, her heart skipped a beat, then resumed at a frantic, giddy pace when she saw Brian's name.

After inhaling a calming breath so she didn't sound too anxious, she set her book aside and connected the call. "Hello?"

"Hey, there," he said in that rich, smooth voice of his.

"I wanted to call you earlier today just to say hi, but things got a little crazy at the clinic and I just got home a little while ago. I hope it's not too late to call?"

"No, not at all." Was he kidding? Just hearing his voice made her feel all warm and fuzzy inside, like a teenager with a huge crush on the cute boy in school. "What happened at the clinic?" she asked, curious to know more about the things he did as a veterinarian.

"There were a lot of dog emergencies today, and two that were accidentally hit by cars, but nothing life-threatening, thank goodness," he said, his tone relieved. "Then, as I was getting ready to leave for the evening, a woman came in with a box of kittens that she'd found abandoned near her work. Normally I would have told her to take them to the animal shelter, but they were already closed and the woman was allergic to cats and couldn't keep them overnight, and I just couldn't turn the kittens away."

Smiling, she pushed her pillows against the headboard and settled more comfortably against them. "You're a softie."

"Yeah, I definitely have a soft spot when it comes to animals," he said unapologetically. "And I have to admit, these kittens were pretty darn cute. I could tell they were starving, so I took them to an enclosed pen I have in the back of the clinic and fed them. Then I went ahead and checked each one of them over to make sure they were healthy."

Of course he had. She could just imagine how gentle he'd been with each kitten, and she'd even bet he'd played with them, too. "Do you have any animals of your own?" she asked.

"No." A regretful sigh drifted over the phone line. "I'd love to have a Golden Retriever, but right now, my schedule at the clinic is so erratic that I just can't give a dog the kind of attention it deserves. When I get married and have kids, we'll definitely have a dog or two, and probably other animals, too."

Thinking about Brian being married with kids made her actually feel...jealous. A ridiculous emotion considering she'd just met him.

"How about you?" he asked, his question bringing her attention back to their conversation. "Any dogs or cats?"

Curling her legs beneath her on the bed, she glanced at the framed photo on her dresser that held a cherished picture of Jayne and her cat, and felt a pang of sadness that thankfully had eased over time. "My aunt gave me a kitten for my tenth birthday. She was white and fluffy and I named her Snowball. She died of old age about six months ago." Jayne still missed the feline every single day.

"I know it's hard. It's like losing a family member." His voice was laced with genuine compassion and understanding. "Have you thought about getting another pet?"

"Sure," she said, but knew it would be difficult to replace her furry friend. "I've thought about going to the animal shelter to adopt a cat, but I'm afraid I'll get there and want to take them all home."

"Now who's the softie?" He chuckled, the deep, masculine sound settling in her belly like a warm shot of cognac.

"Guilty as charged," she admitted.

"So, what were you doing before I called?" he asked, smoothly changing the subject, which she didn't mind.

She ran her fingers over the hardbound book on the comforter beside her. "Just reading the latest thriller from John Connelly."

"Mmm. Sounds exciting."

"Hardly," she said, recalling the gruesome murder scene

she'd been reading that he'd interrupted. "Homicide and serial killers aren't the kind of things that turn me on."

"Thank God," he said humorously. "So tell me, Jayne. What *does* turn you on?"

She wasn't adept at trading innuendos with men, so his flirtatious question caught her by surprise. Normally, she would have shied away from such an intimate discussion, but after Darcie's pep talk that afternoon, she realized this was her chance to test the waters, so to speak.

She plunged in before she changed her mind. "*You* turn me on."

"Good to know," he murmured, an unmistakably wicked note to his voice. "Tell me more."

She bit her bottom lip, feeling just a moment's hesitation. Could she go on and travel down the path this conversation was sure to lead? While engaging in phone sex was a foreign concept to her, the thought of exchanging provocative dialogue with Brian sparked excitement in her belly. Ultimately she trusted Brian and knew he'd never ridicule her attempts, and that knowledge gave her the courage to try.

"That night at the club...I think about it all the time." Her cheeks warmed, but knowing he couldn't see her reaction, she forged on. "It's my go-to fantasy when I need one."

"Mine, too," he said huskily.

His admission bolstered her confidence a little more. Laying her head against the pillows, she closed her eyes and summoned the sexiest memories of that night. "All I have to do is think about your mouth on my breasts, and your fingers touching me..."

"Where?" His voice sounded like crushed gravel. "Where are my fingers touching you?"

Her nipples tightened, and a rush of moisture dampened

her panties, right where she was imagining those long, skillful fingers. Their conversation was quickly turning erotic, her need for Brian building inside her like hot steam that needed release.

And it was easier than she imagined it would be to give him the answer he was waiting for. "Between my legs."

"Yeah," he rasped. "You were so hot and wet."

She pressed her thighs together to ease the ache building there, but it wasn't enough. "You made me that way."

He groaned, the sound vibrating over the line. "You're killing me, sweetheart."

In a good way, she knew. Knowing she could have such an arousing effect on him felt very empowering. "I loved the way you felt thrusting inside of me," she whispered intimately. "You were so hard and thick and I didn't want you to stop."

"You were so tight and eager, and I came a lot sooner than I wanted to."

She bit back a groan of her own and after only a second of uncertainty, she dared to ask, "Are you hard now?"

"Like granite." His breathing was heavy and labored. "And it's all your fault."

She smiled to herself. "I'd say that I'm sorry, but that would be a lie."

"You are so bad."

And bad never felt so good, she realized, surprised at just how easy it had been to be a little naughty with Brian. And how much she'd liked it.

"I need to go," she said reluctantly. It was after eleven and her alarm was set for five. "I have a ton of things to get done at the shop tomorrow and I need to get up early. I'll see you when you pick me up for the rehearsal dinner."

"I can't wait." He sounded anxious *and* impatient.

"Me, either." And she meant it, because as soon as they'd

fulfilled their commitment to Gwen, the rest of the evening belonged solely to the two of them and finishing what they'd started tonight.

# 5

*Who was this woman?*

The question tumbled through Brian's mind as he walked with Jayne to the garden area of the San Diego country club where Gwen's wedding rehearsal was taking place. Between the initiation of phone sex last night, and the sensual way Jayne was dressed now, he was beginning to wonder when she'd become such a self-assured version of herself.

When he'd arrived at Jayne's place to pick her up, he'd been stunned when she'd opened the door wearing a form-fitting pink-and-black dress that accentuated her curves. The top portion of the outfit came to a deep vee between her breasts, displaying a nice amount of pushed up cleavage, and the dress itself wrapped around her gorgeous body and tied off at the waist. The do-me heels were an added bonus that not only boosted her height, but seemed to give a lift to her confidence, as well.

Now, as they made their way to the gazebo where Gwen, Patrick, and a few other people were gathered, his body buzzed with awareness. The light, floral fragrance she wore filled his senses, and each step she took showed a flash of bare, slender leg that drew his gaze every damn time, and made him think about what she might be wearing beneath all that clingy fabric.

If he thought Gwen wouldn't miss them at the rehearsal ceremony and dinner, he would have ushered Jayne back to his car, driven her home, and as soon as they were alone the first thing he'd do was unravel that silky tie at her waist to unwrap her like the delectable gift she was.

But straight ahead, Gwen was waving at the two of them to get their attention. With her arm tucked into her groom-to-be's, she and Patrick both headed in their direction, making an unnoticed escape impossible.

"Jayne, you look lovely," Gwen gushed as she took in Jayne's statuesque appearance, then she glanced at Brian and gave him a once-over, too. "And, of course, you're as handsome as ever, Brian."

"And you are positively glowing," Brian replied to the blushing bride-to-be. He kissed the older woman on the cheek before shaking hands with her fiancé—a distinguished looking man with salt and pepper hair, kind blue eyes, and a likeable personality. "It's good to see you again, Patrick."

"Same here," the other man said with a friendly smile.

Gwen grabbed both of Jayne's hands and held them apart to get a better look at what she was wearing, then gave an approving nod. "I love your new dress and shoes. I think Brian is a good influence on you."

Jayne blushed, and Brian was glad to see that one of his favorite, endearing qualities about Jayne hadn't changed, despite the other transformations she'd made tonight.

"I had nothing to do with her outfit," he insisted.

"Oh, I'm sure you did." Gwen winked at him. "A woman only wears a dress like that to make sure her man's eyes stay on *her* at all times."

"Gwen!"

Jayne tried to admonish the outspoken woman, but Gwen wasn't dissuaded. "It's the truth. I've been around the block a time or two...or five," she admitted, and slanted Patrick a sheepish glance. "I've tried the tactic myself, and it's foolproof."

Brian laughed in amusement. "If that's the case, Jayne's ploy is working. I can't keep my eyes off how stunning she looks." He couldn't keep his hands to himself either, he thought as he slid an arm around her waist and pulled her closer to his side.

Jayne pressed her hands to her pink cheeks and shook her head in embarrassment. "You're both incorrigible."

"It's all in good fun," Brian assured her, knowing she probably hadn't anticipated just how much attention her makeover would draw.

Gwen smiled at the two of them, then shifted her triumphant gaze to Patrick. "Didn't I tell you they'd make an engaging couple?"

"You did." He patted the hand she'd tucked back into the crook of his arm, his eyes filled with pure, unadulterated adoration for the woman he was going to marry. "I'm always telling Gwen that she needs to stop with the matchmaking and blind dates, but she's an incurable romantic and insists that love sometimes needs a little nudge in the right direction to make it happen."

Gwen nodded in agreement. "I just don't ever want anyone to miss out on the greatest love of their life. That almost happened to me, and I'm just so lucky that I got a second chance with Patrick."

An unspoken, emotional look passed between the older couple, a private moment that only they understood and shared.

Someone called out that the rehearsal was about to begin, and Gwen and Patrick headed back to the gazebo where family members were waiting, along with the minister. Brian took a seat with Jayne on one of the white wooden chairs set up on the lawn. A half hour later the practice run for the wedding was over, and Gwen and Patrick introduced them to their children, who were actually older than Jayne and Brian with kids of their own. They mingled for a while and enjoyed a glass of wine and appetizers, then followed the rest of the group inside the country club for dinner.

There were over a dozen people seated at the table, and the conversation around Brian and Jayne was constant and lively, drawing them both into various discussions. But even as Brian talked with the man sitting across from him—who was Patrick's son, Collin—he was one hundred percent aware of everything Jayne said and did.

She was more flirtatious than she'd ever been with him before, and he didn't miss the oh-so-casual way she'd touch her hand to his thigh beneath the table as she asked him a question. Or how she'd purposefully lean into him as she reached for the bread basket, pressing her soft, full breasts against his arm. She whispered in his ear a few times, her husky voice like a caress straight to his groin, and even the way she ate her dinner was an erotic display of throaty moans of pleasure, a wet lick of her lips, and soft, sated sighs that made him think about sex. With her.

Every single move she made, every enchanting surge of laughter that escaped her, every look or touch she gave him, kept his libido at a fever pitch of need.

But there were times, when she thought he wasn't watching her—like now—that he noticed how uncertain and nervous she actually was, as if she wasn't quite sure of her ability to entice him. She was going through the motions, and his body was definitely responding to every single one of her attempts, but through it all he caught glimpses of the sweet, demure woman Jayne was at the very core.

And that was the woman he was ultimately attracted to and wanted.

She glanced up at him, a little startled to find him looking at her, watching her. She'd left her hair down in soft, loose waves, her eyes appeared dark and exotic, and good Lord, he ached for her in physical and emotional ways that defied his own logic or reason.

She tipped her head to the side and sucker punched him in the gut with a sensual smile she'd somehow perfected. "Why do you keep looking at me like that?"

"Because I'm enthralled by you," he replied honestly, and dipped his head closer to hers, to whisper in her ear the way she had in his earlier. "Gwen was right, you know. If your intent was to distract me the entire night with that sexy dress and the way it showcases all your best assets, then I want you to know that I'm totally and completely hooked."

She gave him what he could only interpret as an adorably coy look, but his comment definitely seemed to bolster her confidence. "Good."

Did she really say *good?* He almost chuckled, but didn't want to ruin the moment, or have her think he was ridiculing her. Far from it. He had no idea what she was up to, but he was curious and fascinated enough to go with it and see where it all led.

After dinner, they said their good-byes and Jayne promised to arrive early with all the flowers for the wedding and reception. Once they were sitting in his car with the engine idling, he decided to let Jayne decide what happened next—especially since she seemed to have some kind of agenda tonight. Whatever she wanted to do, he was game.

One hand on the steering wheel and the other on the gear shift, he glanced toward her side of the car. "Is there anything else you'd like to do this evening?"

He watched her take a deep, fortifying breath, then she met his gaze in the darkened interior of the vehicle, her eyes brimming with the same desire pulsing through him. "Yes. I'd like to go back to your place."

*Where the possibilities were absolutely endless,* he thought. "Sure." He kept his reply casual and nonchalant. No stress, no pressure, no expectations. Whatever happened between them once they arrived was totally and completely up to her. Absolutely nothing, or everything she could imagine—he was fine with either as long as it meant spending time with her.

He kept up a steady stream of light, easygoing conversation, mostly about the wedding rehearsal and how much he'd enjoyed meeting Gwen's and Patrick's families. By the time they arrived at his house she appeared much more relaxed, but that calm demeanor seemed to evaporate as soon as they walked into the entryway and he closed and locked the door behind them.

Gently touching his hand to the base of her spine, he guided her into the living room and switched on a lamp. "Would you like a glass of wine, or coffee?"

She shook her head, swallowed hard, and shifted anxiously on her high-heeled shoes. "The only thing I want is you."

Her words came out in a nervous rush of breath, and while his body was immediately on board with her idea, he was hesitant to jump right in until he was certain Jayne had thought things through. "Are you sure you want to do this, Jayne? Because we can just watch TV, or talk—"

"I don't want to talk." She tossed her purse onto the couch, then strolled toward him, the extra sway in her hips drawing his gaze like a magnet. "And I'm sure about *this,* about you and me. *Very* sure."

As he looked one last time into her eyes and saw the

want and hunger darkening their depths, he knew without a doubt her need for him was real and heartfelt, and that's what ultimately swayed him.

With her palm splayed on his chest, she guided him back a few steps, until he found himself pressed against the nearest wall. Immediately, he recognized her move as a role reversal that echoed the night in the stairwell, but this time she was the one in control. Obviously, she felt she had something to prove—to him or herself, he wasn't sure—and for now, for tonight, he was more than willing to let her have her way with him. But later, he intended to make it very clear that she didn't need to try and be something she wasn't with him, that she was everything he wanted and more without changing anything at all.

Then she kissed him, the exquisite feel of her soft, warm mouth against his making him forget everything but her and how much he wanted her. In his bed and in his life. For a very long time. Possibly forever.

The realization made him shudder, and she mistook his reaction for a physical one, instead of the emotional response it had been. He'd correct her error later, because at the moment she was a little busy deepening the connection of their mouths and chasing his tongue with her own while unbuttoning his shirt and pushing it over his shoulders and down his arms. He shrugged out of the garment for her and let it fall to the floor, and her hands quickly dropped to the waistband of his slacks to unbutton his pants.

Just as she started to unzip his trousers, he gently grabbed her wrists, pulled her hands away from his straining cock, and murmured against her lips, "Let's go to the bedroom." He didn't want to do this standing up again. This time, he wanted things horizontal with a soft mattress beneath them.

But he'd forgotten that Jayne was the one in charge,

and she wasn't ready to do things the traditional way. "Not yet," she said, and treated him to a smile that seemed full of feminine secrets. "I want you to sit on the couch."

He reminded himself that it was her show, so he did as she asked. She moved to stand in front of him, and with her teeth grazing her bottom lip and her gaze flickering with a hint of unease that contradicted her next provocative move, she tugged on the tie securing her dress and let it slowly unravel, unerringly heightening the suspense of what lay beneath. Anticipation pumped through Brian's veins, and when the silky fabric finally slid down the length of her body and pooled around her high heeled shoes, his mouth went dry and his cock pulsed with lust and approval.

Her skin turned a rosy shade of pink as he openly and leisurely looked his fill of her, taking in the way the tops of her breasts nearly spilled from the cups of her black lace bra, and how those delicate panties framed her curvy hips and dipped between her supple thighs. He knew it had taken a wealth of courage for her to just stand there while he ravished her with his gaze, and he made sure she knew he liked what he saw. Every…single…inch of her.

Smiling, he forced his gaze back up to her face. "You are so stunning, you take my breath away."

She laughed softly as she knelt between his spread legs. "Darcie did say this lingerie would have that kind of effect on you."

"No, *you* have that kind of effect on me," he said, wanting to clarify the difference. The lingerie did not make her the woman she was on the outside, or even on the inside. She was beautiful, in every way.

She reached to undo his pants, and this time he didn't stop her. He toed off his shoes, then lifted his hips to help her remove his trousers and briefs. She dragged his socks off too, so that he was completely naked. Licking her lips, she shyly appraised his body, and eyed his erection with awe and fascination. Tentatively, she touched the broad head, ran a finger down the rigid length, then wrapped her hand snug around his shaft as she boldly explored that male part of him.

*Jesus.* His cock twitched and the muscles in his stomach rippled as he endured the overwhelming pleasure of having her hands on him...then her mouth as she unexpectedly leaned forward, wrapped her lips around him, and took him deep. A ragged groan erupted from his chest, and instinctively, his hips jerked upward. His hands fisted in her hair—at first to show her what he liked, then to pull her away when he discovered she was a natural at giving blow jobs and knew just how to push him to the brink of no return.

He tugged her head gently, and exhaled a relieved stream of breath when she finally released him. "I need a condom," he rasped. "They're in the bedroom."

"I have one in my purse." She reached for the bag she'd tossed on the couch earlier and retrieved a foil packet.

So, just like the first time, she'd come prepared. This all suddenly felt too familiar, like a repeat of the past somehow, but before he could analyze the feeling she was standing and skimming out of her panties and urging him to put the condom on.

As soon as the latex was in place, she straddled his hips and sank down on him, until he was buried to the hilt inside of her. Then she went utterly still. Eyes wide, she stared at him expectantly, hesitantly, every one of her doubts and insecurities laid bare for him to see.

He smoothed his palms up her thighs, then traveled higher, to the indentation of her waist. "There's no way to get this wrong, sweetheart," he murmured, and slowly guided her hips back and forth, again and again, so that she could feel the slide of his cock deep inside. "Just do whatever feels good. Slow and easy, or hard and fast, you're in charge," he reminded her.

Placing her hands on his shoulders, she adopted the same rhythm he'd created, slowly undulating her hips against his, then gradually picking up the pace until he was rubbing that sweet spot within her and she was completely lost in sensation. Moaning rapturously, she closed her eyes, tossed her head back and arched into him, taking him deeper still.

The straps of her bra fell down her arms, and her full, naked breasts spilled free, beckoning him with a temptation he couldn't resist. He palmed the weight of one warm breast in his hand, opened his mouth over the other, and used his teeth and tongue to finesse her nipple. She felt and tasted like heaven, and he couldn't get enough of her. Didn't know if he ever would.

She continued to ride him, and he knew the exact moment her orgasm surged through her. She cried out as her inner muscles clenched him tight, milked him, and he gripped her hips tighter, groaning as he came right along with her, his heart racing like a man who'd stepped off a very steep cliff with no net to catch him.

It felt like he'd taken a freefall…straight into love.

As he tried to catch his breath, he realized that the knowledge didn't shock him. Instead, he welcomed the feeling, and hoped she would, too.

Once he recovered, mentally and physically, he looked at Jayne to gauge how she was doing. Her head was tipped forward, but her eyes were still closed, as if she wasn't quite ready to face him just yet. But her expression was sated, and she had a small, pleased smile on her lips. Her bare breasts were still distracting as hell, and he slipped the straps back up to her shoulders so she was covered once again.

"Open your eyes and look at me, Jayne," he said, tucking her tousled hair behind her ear so he could see her face.

Her lashes slowly drifted upward and her gaze met his. An intimate warmth and affection glowed in the brown depths, and it was all he needed to see to know she'd been affected, too. She might have started out this evening believing it was all about sex, but she wasn't immune to the deeper connection between them.

He grinned at her. "I like this confident, sexy Jayne."

He'd meant it as a huge compliment, but instead of basking in the accolade the smile on her lips faded and the light in her eyes dimmed, and he wasn't sure why.

She moved off of him and he let her because he sensed she needed a few moments to herself. While she stepped back into her panties, he picked up his briefs from the floor, then made a quick trip to the bathroom. When he returned, she'd slipped back into her dress and was securing the tie at her waist.

Not a good sign, he thought.

"I should go," she said, and wouldn't meet his gaze.

In the short time he'd been gone the warm afterglow of sex had evaporated. She'd clearly withdrawn and erected emotional walls. Remembering the abrupt way she'd bolted on him that night at the club, a feeling of foreboding settled in the pit of his stomach.

Trying not to overreact, he braced his hands on his hips. "I'd like you to stay."

"I CAN'T." SOMEHOW, SOMEWAY, Jayne managed to remain calm as she picked up her purse, her gaze still averted. She feared once she looked him in the eye she'd unravel and fall to pieces, and that wouldn't be a pretty sight at all. "Tomorrow's Valentine's Day, and it's going to be crazy busy at the shop."

"I'm off tomorrow," he said, obviously hearing her reply for the excuse it was and calling her on it. "I'll come and help out at the shop with whatever you need until we have to get ready for Gwen's wedding."

"I'd rather you didn't," she said, and finally forced herself to look at him.

She saw the confusion etching his features, and sure enough, her heart clenched like a vise in her chest. A sure sign that she was in much deeper than she'd ever anticipated, and that scared her on a level so emotional it nearly stole the breath from her lungs.

As did his heartfelt comment about liking the sexy, adventurous Jayne who'd seduced him tonight. She'd heard the approval and awe in his voice, and deep inside she'd been unable to shake the lingering fear that *the real Jayne*—the one who'd been raised by an aunt who would have disapproved of her wanton behavior tonight—wasn't bold and daring enough to keep a man like Brian content and satisfied in the bedroom for the long term.

The truth was, she was way out of her league with Brian, and risking a relationship with him had the huge potential of leaving him disappointed with her, as well. Especially if she couldn't live up to his expectations of the kind of sexually experienced woman he thought she should be.

She'd wanted one more night with him, and it had been amazing—another hot memory to store away to fantasize about when she was alone. But she knew that ending things now, as difficult as it might be, was for the best and would undoubtedly save her a wealth of heartache later.

Brian stabbed his fingers through his hair in frustration, his brows creased into a dark frown. "I'm not sure what's going on here, Jayne. Was it something I said or did?"

She winced at the sharp note to his voice. "I can't do this," she whispered around the lump in her throat.

"Can't do what?" he pushed.

"Be with you." Swallowing hard, she pressed a hand to her stomach, a feeling of dread nearly overwhelming her, because she was about to push the most exciting man she'd ever met out of her life for good. "That confident, sexy Jayne you say you like so much isn't really me. And deep down inside, I'm not really the kind of girl who goes around having sex with strangers in a darkened stairwell."

"And I don't want a woman who has sex with every single guy she meets," he refuted with a shake of his head. "I know you're not *that* kind of girl. I knew the night we first met you were different, that you didn't do that kind of thing easily. And one more thing," he went on, clearly not done with his argument. "This is not about you having to be that confident, sexy, over-the-top person in order to hold my interest. This is about you and me and the connection between us. That's what matters, and we have *great* chemistry together."

Jayne wanted to believe him. She really, truly did. But when it came to the kind of scorching hot passion they'd shared, she found it difficult to trust that something so sexually phenomenal and emotionally gratifying could last into the future.

The burn of tears filled her eyes, and she hated that her emotions and fears kept her from taking the biggest risk of all with Brian. "I…can't."

He looked completely and utterly defeated. "You mean you won't," he said, his tone flat.

She didn't reply, because there was nothing left to say that could change her mind, and he seemed to sense that, as well.

He drove her back home in silence, but there was no denying that he looked angry and hurt, and she felt responsible for both. He walked her to her front door and made sure she was safely inside before turning and leaving without so much as a goodbye.

She knew she deserved Brian's cool attitude after the way she'd just cut him out of her life, and as she watched through the living room window as he drove away, she'd never felt so alone.

# 6

VALENTINE'S DAY was filled with love and romance, hearts and flowers, and secret admirers and passionate lovers. The moment Jayne opened the doors to her shop that morning she'd been bombarded by those sentiments, and was reminded with every flower, card, stuffed animal and balloon bouquet she'd sold that she was spending yet another Valentine's Day alone.

*This year, by her own choice.*

She'd had a lover and could have been basking in the knowledge that she had someone special to share the day with, but instead her heart felt empty, hollow, even. Like she'd lost something precious and rare. The pain of walking away from Brian was more intense than she'd ever anticipated, but her fear of rejection was even stronger and that was what had kept her from staying with Brian last night.

She'd honestly believed she could have a one-night fling with Brian and walk away with her heart intact, but that hadn't been the case. Because while she'd believed her seduction would just be about hot sex, she'd been flooded with emotions that were new and terrifying and had shaken her to the core.

Last night, she'd learned that she wasn't the kind of person who could separate the two into nice little compartments, and as soon as she realized that she'd fallen for Brian, and fallen hard, old fears had clawed their way to the surface and she'd panicked.

And now she was all alone. Again.

Sighing, she pushed the troubling thoughts from her mind and kept busy with the steady stream of customers that came into the shop throughout the afternoon. But there was no escaping the love, laughter and overall happiness everyone seemed to be feeling. Even Darcie's boyfriend dropped by to give her a large heart-shaped box of her favorite chocolates, and nestled inside had been a diamond engagement ring.

In front of everyone in the shop, Josh had gotten down on one knee and proposed to the woman he loved, and with a squeal of excitement, Darcie had said yes. Cheers and clapping ensued, and Jayne hugged her best friend and congratulated her.

While she was thrilled for Darcie, all the romance in the air made Jayne feel like she was suffocating. Needing a break, she went back to her office where it was quiet and pulled out some paperwork. A little while later, someone knocked on the closed door, then Darcie poked her head inside with a big, I'm-so-in-love grin.

"Guess what?" she asked, her eyes still sparkling with joy over her recent proposal.

"You're in love and engaged?" Jayne replied, her voice light and teasing.

"Yeah, I am. But that's not all." Darcie stepped inside, a pink box tucked beneath her arm. "Something just arrived for you."

Surprise and curiosity rippled through Jayne as she stared at the box, which had little cut-out holes in it and a heart on top with the words "Be Mine" written across. "Who is it from?"

"I don't know. A courier dropped it off." Darcie gently set the box on Jayne's desk. "Open it up and find out."

"Okay." Just as she reached for the lid, she heard a soft, mewling sound from inside, and her heart skipped a beat. She opened the box and staring up at her was the sweetest, cutest, fluffiest black and white kitten with the deepest green eyes. Immediately, Jayne knew who the feline was from, and as she lifted the ball of fur from the box she noticed there was a card attached to the big red bow tied loosely around the kitten's neck.

Cuddling the kitten to her chest, she read the bold, masculine print on the card.

She needed a good home and I thought of you. I know you'll take good care of her. Her love and acceptance is unconditional, as is mine. Love, Brian.

"Oh, I am so in love," Darcie gushed as she scratched the kitten beneath its chin.

So was Jayne. With the cat and with Brian. She swallowed the huge lump in her throat and smiled as the cat began to purr—loudly. "You're already taken," she said to Darcie.

"So I am." She sighed and glanced at the diamond solitaire on her ring finger. "By the way, the courier also left a box of cat food and other supplies for your new friend. I'll have someone bring them back for you."

"Thanks."

Once Darcie was gone, Jayne played with the kitten for a while, then realized she needed to figure out a name for the feline, but nothing clever sprang to mind. She also thought about what Brian had written on the card, about the cat's love and acceptance being unconditional…as was his—despite the fact that she'd so carelessly, and selfishly, walked away from him last night.

Brian's words haunted her for the rest of the afternoon, until it was time for Jayne to leave. She boxed up the flowers for Gwen's wedding and reception, then went home to take a shower and change. She made a nice bed for her kitten in the laundry room and left her with a litter box, food and water, then headed to the country club on her own.

The fact that Jayne arrived for the wedding alone didn't escape Gwen's notice. As soon as Jayne was finished setting up the flowers and arrangements, she met with Gwen in the bridal room, the other woman looking concerned when she should have been happy and glowing.

"Where's Brian?" Gwen asked without preamble. She was sitting at a vanity table, dressed in white lace and looking like the beautiful bride she was going to be, while her bridesmaids continued to primp and get ready for the ceremony. "The two of you were supposed to come to the wedding together. What happened?"

Jayne knew the woman's questioning was inevitable, and she did her best to explain the situation without going into detail. "We decided to come separately."

"Why?" Gwen frowned. "Did the two of you have a spat?"

Jayne pulled a clear plastic container from her purse that contained a special something for Gwen. "More like a difference of opinion," she hedged.

Gwen waved a regal hand in the air. "Then talk it out and make it work."

"I wish it was that simple."

"It is," Gwen said matter-of-fact, then lowered her voice a fraction so only Jayne could hear. "And the best part is, the make-up sex is amazing."

Jayne laughed at the older woman's outrageous comment. At sixty-eight, Gwen was feisty as heck. "I made something especially for you."

Gwen wagged a finger at her. "You're changing the subject."

"Yes, I am." She didn't want to talk about Brian any more. It hurt too much. "It's a floral hairpin," she said, and showed her the cluster of fragrant roses and gardenias she'd designed.

"It's gorgeous," Gwen said, truly touched by the gesture. "Will you put it in my hair for me?"

"Sure." Smiling, Jayne used the attached comb to secure the flowers into Gwen's upswept hair, then pinned it in place.

Gwen looked into the vanity mirror, her expression softening. "Today I'm going to marry the man I should have married fifty years ago."

Jayne did the math and realized fifty years ago Gwen would have been eighteen. Gwen had always referred to Patrick as the love of her life, but Jayne didn't know the story behind their meeting and courtship. "What do you mean?" she asked.

"Sit down." Gwen patted the chair next to her, and once Jayne was comfortable, she went on. "I've never told you why I've been married and divorced so many times."

"It's really none of my business."

"I know that, but I want to tell you, because sometimes we lose sight of what's really important to us, like I did." Gwen glanced up, and her gaze took on a faraway look. "Patrick and I were both sixteen when we met, and we were young and madly in love and I thought we'd get married once I graduated from school. But my parents never approved of Patrick. We were wealthy, and his family was not, and my father wanted 'better' for me, and that's what he told Patrick when he went to my father to ask for my hand in marriage when I turned eighteen."

Jayne could only imagine how shocked and hurt Patrick had been, and by the pained look on Gwen's face, she'd been devastated, too.

"So, Patrick broke up with me and joined the Army, and I went on to be the dutiful daughter, and after a while Patrick and I completely lost touch." Gwen smiled sadly. "The first man I married was a doctor, but he wasn't Patrick. None of my four husbands were, hence the divorces. I spent all those years searching for that same connection I felt with Patrick, and even though we both went on to marry other people and have our own families, none of the other men I was with matched up. Patrick was the only one who accepted me for who I was inside, and not for my family's wealth, and I let him go and never even tried to fight for him and what we had together, and I should have. All those wasted years..." Gwen shook her head in regret.

The emotion in Gwen's voice prompted Jayne to take the other woman's hand in hers and give it a gentle squeeze. Obviously, Gwen's story had a happy ending, but it had taken many years for Gwen and Patrick to find one another again via a social networking site. But now Jayne had a better understanding of Gwen's need to play matchmaker and set people up. She wanted them to have their happily-ever-after, just like she'd gotten hers.

Jayne also realized that her Aunt Millie had been so wrong about Gwen. Gwen wasn't wanton...she was passionate and loving and hopeful. She was a strong, confident woman who enjoyed everything life had to offer and wasn't afraid of following her dreams, which included sharing the rest of her years with the man who'd stolen her heart fifty years ago.

"I know this sounds crazy, but I see myself and Patrick

in you and Brian. You two are slight opposites, but it's obvious to me that you also have a special connection, and that's worth taking a chance on."

*Connection.* There was that word again. Brian had used it, too. And they did *connect,* on so many different levels it was frightening to her. He was the first man to accept her completely, quirks and all, and as scared as she might be to hand her heart over to Brian, it was time to take a leap of faith and trust in Brian and what was between them.

*Faith.* She smiled, realizing what a perfect name that would make for her new kitten.

"The wedding is starting in five minutes," someone called out, and Jayne knew that was her cue to leave. She gave Gwen a hug, and before they parted ways Gwen shared one more piece of advice, and that was to follow her heart. Jayne promised her she would.

After leaving the bridal suite, Jayne took a seat on one of the white wooden lawn chairs just minutes before the ceremony music began. As the wedding party took their places in the lit-up gazebo, Jayne's gaze anxiously searched the small crowd of people, looking for Brian. She didn't find him, and a part of her wondered if he'd decided not to come tonight, then she discarded that idea. Despite what might have happened between the two of them, Brian wouldn't disappoint Gwen.

Once the ceremony was over, everyone filtered back into one of the country club's ballrooms for the reception. It was then, on the other side of the rows of chairs that she finally saw Brian. Her pirate. The man who'd swept her off her feet and hopefully still wanted her. He looked gorgeous, and her eyes ate him up, taking in his tousled dark hair, his crisp white shirt, and the perfect fit of his navy suit.

His gaze locked on hers, and her heart leapt into her

throat and her palms were suddenly sweaty. She forced her feet to walk toward him, and the sense of longing that filled her felt so, so right. Only with this man, she realized.

Because he was *the one*. From the depths of her heart, she knew it. And believed it.

She stopped in front of him, her stomach churning, because she had no idea what was going through that head of his after what she'd put him through last night.

"I'm so sorry," she blurted, needing to get this out before she lost her nerve. "I'm sorry I walked out last night. I'm sorry I was too scared to stay. All I know is that I'm following my heart now, and it's leading me straight to you." And she knew it always would.

"I don't want to lose you," she rushed on, her voice sandpaper rough. "And I don't want to spend years regretting the fact that I let you go. Can you forgive me for being so stupid?"

The corner of his mouth quirked up in a charming, relieved grin. "There's nothing to forgive, sweetheart," he said, his tone rife with understanding as he reached out and caressed the back of his fingers against her cheek. "I know you're scared and I figured you needed time to process everything. There was no way I was going to let you walk away for good, because you're worth fighting for."

She shook her head, wondering how she'd gotten so lucky with him. Oh, yeah, Gwen and her blind date. "Are you for real?" she teased.

"I think so." He reached for her and pulled her into his embrace. "But come here and you tell me."

Completely alone with him out in the garden area, she wrapped her arms around his neck, his body warm and solid against hers. And very, very real. "You are everything I've ever wanted, and more," she told him, and knew there was one request she needed to ask of him. "This connection of ours is all so new to me, so please be patient with me."

His hand stroked down her back and over her bottom, his eyes darkening with desire for her. "It's new to me, too," he confessed huskily. "I've never fallen in love with anyone so fast before."

"Love?" Shocked, the word caught in her throat.

"Yeah, love." For a moment, he looked uncertain, and his hold on her tightened, as if he feared she'd try and bolt again. "Are you okay with that?"

Hope formed in her chest, and she embraced it. "More than okay." She exhaled a deep breath, and trusting him to be there for her always, she returned the sentiment that had been blossoming in her heart. "I love you, too."

With an answering groan, he kissed her, pressing their mouths together in an intense, fierce meeting of souls. His tongue glided past her lips, and his hands slid into her hair to hold her steady so he could drink his fill of her. When he finally lifted his head, she was breathless and aroused and wishing they were alone.

"By the way. Thank you for my Valentine's Day gift. I already love her," she said of the precious kitten he'd given her.

He smiled, his hands still skimming her body, as if he couldn't stop touching her. "I knew you would. What did you name her?"

"Faith."

"Really?" He sounded surprised. "Any special reason why you chose that name?"

She nodded, her fingers undoing the first few buttons on his shirt so she could slip her hands inside and feel the heat of his skin against her palms. "Because every time I see her I'm going to think that I need to have faith in my life. Faith in you. Faith in us."

"I like that," he whispered. "A lot."

She bit her bottom lip and eyed the darkened gazebo behind them. Music poured out of the reception area, and they were still all alone. Dusk had turned to twilight, casting strategic shadows in the flowered arbor, and the romantic atmosphere gave Jayne a very naughty idea.

"Do you think anyone would miss us if we disappeared into that gazebo for fifteen minutes or so?" she asked huskily.

He arched a brow at her brazen suggestion, but the lusty grin tipping the corners of his mouth told her that he liked her way of thinking. "I think it's safe. Everybody's having too much fun inside."

Willing to take the risk, she led him into the white structure and proceeded to get acquainted with just how mind-blowing make-up sex could be. And how a bit of spontaneity could add a whole lot of spice to their love life.

Because with Brian, she felt daring and adventurous and wild. It wasn't something she had to force or pretend with him…it just was.

\* \* \* \* \*

# HOLD ON
## Leslie Kelly

To Denise Damiano and all the rest
of the "old gang" at Answerphone—
it was lots of fun!

# 1

SARAH HOLT'S JOB might not be the most exciting one in the world, but it sure could be sexy. Like right now, for instance.

She'd just heard personal details about someone else's sex life. Soon, she'd share those details with a rich, powerful man. They'd discuss private, naughty things. There'd be mentions of heat and odd sensations in personal areas. The word *intercourse* might enter the conversation, and *vagina* certainly would.

Sexy stuff.

Except for the fact that the man she'd be speaking to was sixty and married, that the heat was caused by fever and the odd sensations involved itching. Oh, plus, the intercourse was being had by—and the vagina belonged to—another woman.

Yeah, super-sexy, that. Only, *not*. But all in a day's work—if you worked as an answering-service operator for a company that specialized in taking after-hours calls for physicians. Or, in her case, if you were the co-owner of Call Anytime, who doubled as an operator during heavy shifts like this one.

Her business partner, Mindy, sat in their office doing

paperwork. Sarah, who had lost the coin toss, was here in the bullpen taking forty calls an hour. Which was why she had just had the pleasure of hearing an itchy, hot-crotched woman describe her symptoms…as if getting *that* personal would ensure a return call from her physician.

"So you'll get Dr. Emerson to call me back?" asked the woman who'd dialed her doctor's number on this busy Saturday. "Valentine's Day is Monday, and I've got a date."

*Poor guy. Hope he practices safe sex.*

Before the caller had finished describing her symptoms, Sarah had pulled up Dr. Emerson's after-hours instructions on her work station. As usual, he wanted to be paged to call the service to get all the gory details, rather than receiving them in a text.

"I'll page him and give him your message."

"So, he'll call me right back?" the woman persisted.

Knowing not to promise that, Sarah repeated, "I'll page him."

Hanging up, she sent the page, then eyed the dedicated doctor's line, which every operator could access but only senior ones were supposed to answer. She was the most senior person on the floor…and would almost certainly be the one stuck talking to Dr. Emerson about his yeasty patient. *Oh, yay.*

As Sarah waited for the doctor to respond—certain he'd call from a golf course—aka every Florida doctor's second home—she forced herself to remember it was good that she had to work the phones today. It meant business was thriving.

For the past two years, she and Mindy had worked sixty-hour weeks, both of them determined to succeed. Having been best friends since the second grade, when Mindy had rescued Sarah's Smurfette backpack from a classroom bully, they made a good team.

Mindy had always been the tough, ballsy, backpack-saver, while Sarah was the quiet, reasonable one who could be counted on to talk her friend out of doing something stupid. Going into business together had seemed like a no-brainer. Mindy provided the creative juices and Sarah the business sense. And after just two years, Call Anytime was a bona-fide success.

Of course, that business success had caused some erosion in other areas. Her personal life was in a stall. And her romantic one in a kamikaze death spiral.

*Be honest…it wasn't like you had one to begin with.*

"Doctors' line!" someone called, interrupting her musings.

She answered. As expected, it was Dr. Emerson, who listened, flirted, then hung up as someone in the background called, "Fore!" Sighing at how repetitive the days seemed, she decided to take a quick break, but paused when she saw an incoming call pop up on her work station.

"Somebody's calling Dr. Steve," she whispered. It was fitting that Steve Wilshire was a cardiologist—just seeing his name on the screen made her heart race.

Like Dr. Emerson, Dr. Wilshire liked to phone in for his messages. So, if this was a legitimate patient issue, he'd be paged, and somebody here would get to talk to him soon.

Her heart raced even faster.

Dr. Steve had the greatest voice, deep and calm, masculine and sexy. He'd made quite an impression on her during their very first conversation. He was incredibly friendly and easygoing when calling in, unlike a lot of other high-powered doctors. Never slimy, never inappropriate, never rude and abrupt—he was simply a gentleman. One who always sounded truly concerned about his patients.

From that first call, she had wanted to meet him in

person, something she'd never even considered before. Some devilish bit of curiosity had even made her look him up online.

*Big mistake.* Seeing his handsome picture on his website had almost made her too self-conscious to answer when he called. But, knowing they'd never meet face to face, she had let herself enjoy the brief verbal interactions—titillating highlights of some pretty boring days.

It was innocent and harmless. She'd never let on that she had a tiny crush on him, or that she fantasized that one day he'd ask if he could take her to dinner so they could meet at last. Their relationship was built on her lonely daydreams, she knew that…but that didn't mean it wasn't important to her. And though she knew he would remain in her daydreams, there was one thing she'd done differently when talking to Steve Wilshire. She'd let him hear the *real* her.

After surviving a shocking bout with esophageal cancer as a child, which had damaged her vocal cords, Sarah had been left with an unusual speaking voice. As an adult, the suggestion that she become a phone sex operator had grown so frequent, she'd considered changing her name to Desirée or Erotique. Yet, it was because of her voice that she and Mindy had come up with the idea for this business. Smooth and throaty could be sexy, but it could also be soothing, especially to frantic patients.

Soothing…except when she was talking to Steve Wilshire. Whenever *he* called in, she probably sounded like that vampy phone-sex operator everyone said she should be. She pretended she was the kind of woman who could *have* a man like that, rather than one who'd been so sheltered by her parents throughout her sickly childhood that she wasn't far past the virgin state. At twenty-five. Pathetic.

Four rings now. *Too long.* Unable to resist, she pushed

the answer button, saying, "Dr. Wilshire's answering service."

A woman's voice—airy, vapid—replied, "Hi. Uh, I have a problem. I mean, it's not a medical thing…it's personal."

Disappointment filled her. "The doctor requires any non-emergency calls to be made to his office when it opens Monday."

"He might wanna know I'm breaking our blind date tonight."

A blind date? The incredibly handsome doctor needed to be set up on a blind date two days before Valentine's Day? That was beyond wrong. And the very idea that someone was breaking that date, through an answering service no less, was even more so.

"But I guess you could leave the message for Monday, so he'll know why I didn't show up," the woman said, unconcerned.

Indignant, Sarah snapped, "I'll take the message."

"Okay. I met this other guy last night." Squealing, the woman added, "He's a rodeo clown and he's takin' me to Texas!"

A prize, indeed. "Okay."

"The doc won't care," she said carelessly. "We've never met. It was just a set-up through a friend of a friend."

Some friend. Sounded like Dr. Steve needed a new one. Stat.

Biting her tongue, Sarah took the whole message, sighing when she got the woman's name. Bambi. Just perfect. A bimbo named Bambi had definitely never been part of her sweet—and yes, a little erotic—daydreams about Dr. Steven Wilshire.

Sarah managed a somewhat polite goodbye before hanging up and paging the doctor. But she did not want to be the one to deliver this message. She might sound too personally upset on his behalf...because she was. Wonderful, handsome men like Dr. Steve shouldn't get dumped before the first date. It was against the laws of nature.

Pulling off her headset, she glanced at the operator in the next chair. "I'm going on break," she said, before heading into the glass-walled office she shared with Mindy.

Knowing Sarah better than anyone, her friend must have immediately noticed something was wrong. "What is it?" Mindy asked with a concerned frown.

"Some twit was supposed to meet Dr. Steve tonight for a blind date, and she canceled on him with two hours notice."

Mindy rolled her eyes, stating the obvious. "She obviously hasn't seen him."

No doubt about that, even if the woman hadn't confirmed it herself. "She said they never laid eyes on each other."

"Her loss." Mindy smiled that Cheshire-cat smile. "If I'd known he was on the market, I'd have made you take a shot."

Sarah sputtered a little, feeling heat flood her face. She had never said a word to anyone about her secret fantasies.

"You think I didn't notice you had the hots for the guy?"

"Oh, God," she groaned.

"You can't hide lust from me, chica. I invented it."

That wasn't too much of an exaggeration. Mindy had also likely invented, or at least inspired, the term *maneater*. And yes, Sarah supposed there was lust to see. But what she felt went further than that. True, she was attracted to Steve Wilshire, but she also just liked him. A lot. A whole lot.

Maybe she'd built him up to be more than he was—like some kind of Prince Charming. But in her fairy tales, the charming prince didn't get ditched by some rodeo-clown-loving airhead.

"So, a blind date… You're sure they've never seen each other before?"

"I'm sure. Why?" Sarah asked.

Before Mindy could answer, the dedicated physicians-only line rang. To her surprise, Mindy answered it. "Doctors' line," she said, her eyes on Sarah.

Tensing, Sarah watched, wondering why Mindy had answered. Things weren't *that* crazy out in the bullpen.

"We did page you, Dr. Wilshire," her friend said. "But it's not a 911. The woman you're supposed to meet tonight called."

Closing her eyes, Sarah mentally filled in the other half of the conversation. *I didn't want to date her anyway. Where's that sexy-voiced angel who usually answers my calls?*

"She forgot where you're supposed to meet."

Her eyes flying open, Sarah mouthed, "What are you doing?"

"She asked me to text her the address. Oh, and she also wanted to know how you are going to recognize each other?"

Sarah leaned closer to whisper, "Are you crazy?"

Jotting something down, Mindy said, "Okay, doc, we're all set. I'll send her the info right away." Then she hung up.

"What are you thinking?" Sarah snapped. "Do you want us to lose one of our best clients?" The idea of losing even that small vocal connection with her fantasy man made her head hurt. Not to mention her heart.

"It's true, they've never met. He said he'd be wearing

a navy suit and she should look for him by the fountain." Mindy shoved the paper she'd written on across the desk. "Here's the address." She grinned. "You have two hours."

Getting it, Sarah's jaw dropped. "You've lost your mind."

"Oh, come on, it's perfect. He has no idea what the woman he's meeting looks like. So, you take this chick's place, have a great time, get laid by your dreamboat and walk away."

*Get laid by your dreamboat.* The words echoed in her head, even though "getting laid" by him had never even entered her mind.

Making love? Well…she'd cop to that, if only to herself.

"Hell, I'd do it in a heartbeat," Mindy added.

All the more reason why she shouldn't. Mindy's love-'em-and-leave-'em track record wasn't exactly stellar. "I can't."

"You can. You're beautiful and sexy and smart… You're the only one who doesn't know that yet." Smirking, she added, "And if you don't do it, I will."

Sarah gasped. "You do and I'll rip your hair out."

The look on Mindy's face told her she'd been manipulated into revealing how she felt about Steve Wilshire. Damn.

But it was true. She did want him, even if they hadn't met face to face. *Doesn't matter. You can't do it. You* won't *do it.*

Only, as the minutes ticked by, Sarah began to suspect that she could do it. And, more shockingly…that she *would*.

STANDING BY THE FOUNTAIN in the lobby of an upscale beachfront hotel, Steve Wilshire glanced at his watch. His date was late—only ten minutes, but still, enough to make him worry.

What had he been thinking, letting Rick set him up? His old buddy had been married and divorced *three* times. That was two times more than Steve's pathetic attempt at matrimony. So what had compelled him to take the other man's advice and dive back into the shark-filled waters called dating?

Then he remembered. Dr. Graham Tate—older, proper, a bit stodgy…and his potential partner. The desire to form a partnership with another doctor—relieving the heavy weight of a solo practice from his shoulders—had led him here. Tate was a family man. And when Steve saw him tonight, he did not want to be asked, yet again, why he'd ever divorced that lovely Jenny.

*Because lovely Jenny was a lying, conniving schemer?*

True, but that wasn't a very good answer. Bringing a date would stop the questions and signal that he was not a sap pining for his ex-wife. Mainly because he *wasn't*…pining, anyway. Yeah, the break-up had stung, but looking back and being honest, he knew his own inattentiveness had at least contributed to it.

And if he ended up in bed with this woman, Bambi, who according to Rick would be the perfect person to get him 'back in the saddle,' all the better. No-strings sex with a party girl might be just what the doctor ordered.

Still, a blind date with a woman he'd never even spoken to? "You must have been out of your mind!"

"Excuse me, you're Steve Wilshire, aren't you?" said a woman, a *very* sexy-voiced one, who had come up unnoticed and had obviously overheard him talking to himself.

*Great way to start the evening. She thinks you're loco.*

Sighing, he turned to her. "Yeah, sorry, uh…"

The words died on his lips because she was *so* not who he'd been expecting to see. She was nowhere near the type of woman Rick would ever set him up with. She was too smart-looking, quietly pretty, not flashy enough for his old buddy.

Though she suited him just fine. *Very fine indeed.*

She smiled. And she went from pretty to breathtaking. "Hi."

"Hi," he replied, the breath sucked out of him by that warm smile, and the twinkle it brought to a pair of amazing bronze eyes.

Then there was the voice. God, that sexy, smooth, whiskey-soaked-velvet voice. He wanted to listen to her read pages from the phone book. And if he thought he might get to hear her whisper wicked, erotic words in his ear as he made love to her, he would happily lead her out of here to some place more private, to hell with the fundraiser, with Tate, with the partnership.

He'd never had such a strong, sudden reaction to a woman before, and he almost chalked it up to pure sexual deprivation. But he didn't think that was it. He met women every day, and since his divorce a lot of them had made their interest known. Some of them had been damned attractive, too. But not one had really gotten his juices flowing with just a few words.

*Don't get too excited, jackass. Your real date's gonna be here any minute.*

Right. She wasn't his date—she couldn't be. Frustration and disappointment washed over him and he forced himself to get his head out of his pants. Or her panties.

Mistake. Thinking of her panties almost put a tent in those pants of his. He clenched his teeth and willed his cock back into Idle. Hell, he was reacting like some fifteen-year-old kid meeting a hot college girl for the first time.

"You are Steve Wilshire, right?"

He nodded, wondering what she wanted. Because, as much as he might like to walk into the banquet with this woman on his arm, he knew she wasn't here for that. Obviously she recognized him from somewhere and had approached him for another reason.

*Please don't be some surgeon's trophy wife.*

The thought made him shift his gaze to her left hand. No ring. *Whew.*

Before he could ask her what he could do for her, she shocked him completely. "I'm your blind date."

He was momentarily struck dumb, all his expectations, his certainties, fleeing in a pleased rush. It didn't make any sense, but for just a second, he didn't really care. His pulse sped up a little, a pure adrenaline reaction to excitement.

Yeah. Excitement. Interest. Heat.

Intense curiosity.

She swallowed hard, lifted her chin, and stuck out a hand. Her plump bottom lip trembled the tiniest bit before she said, "It's nice to meet you."

"Uh, you, too," he murmured, taking her hand, still not quite understanding any of this.

She *had* just said she was his date, right? This petite, pretty rather than in-your-face-sexy woman with thick, honey-brown hair that brushed soft-looking bare shoulders, was his date? The woman with *that* voice was his date?

Wouldn't that be nice…if it were really true.

"I'm sorry I'm a little late," she said.

God, that voice. It brought forth every one of his boyhood Jessica Rabbit fantasies. It also sounded vaguely familiar…but probably because every guy dreamed of being set up with a woman who looked like sweetness and sounded like sin.

There was, of course, one problem.

"I didn't mean to keep you waiting."

"It's okay," he mumbled, still holding on to her hand, which she made no attempt to pull from his grasp.

Her fingers were soft, small, like the rest of her. But she was no waif. She had curves where a woman should be curved, and perfectly indented valleys that invited a man's hands. Those perfect curves and valleys were perfectly displayed in her strapless black dress.

He'd been expecting a tall, stacked, leggy, vapid blond bimbo and had gotten a short, curvy, brunette, whiskey-voiced mystery woman.

Not knowing what to say, or even what to think, he simply continued to stare, reaffirming his first impressions.

Yes, petite. Yes, adorably sexy. Yes, honey-brown hair, beautiful gleaming eyes, creamy skin, bare shoulders, amazingly sexy voice. Yes, incredibly hot.

And, no. She most definitely was not his date.

He'd seen a picture of the woman Rick had set him up with. Actually, he'd seen several. Bambi's Facebook page had contained a bunch of images. Many of them, he suspected, had been taken by her, courtesy of one extended arm—the new standard portraiture of the social-networking age.

This woman looked absolutely nothing like that collagen-lipped, platinum blonde, who, according to her profile, liked kittycats and words that started with the letter *S*.

Right now, looking at this imposter, a few *S* words came to mind. Words like *stroke. Slide. Squeeze.* And they grew even more graphic from there.

Funny, he hadn't had any of those wicked thoughts when he'd seen the pictures on his laptop screen. So, no, he was not disappointed at this last-minute substitution. Not one bit.

But he couldn't help wondering...if this *wasn't* the woman Rick had set him up with, who was she?

And what the hell was she up to?

## 2

*You shouldn't have done this.*

The words had been replaying in Sarah's head since the moment she'd spied Steve across the lobby. They had replaced the ones that had been rolling through her head during her drive home from work, her quick shower, her frantic search through her closet and the drive up the coast to this hotel: *You're not going to do this.*

Now, however, seeing the warm smile, the interest in his face, another phrase began to whisper. *This just might work.*

What that meant, what would define "success," she couldn't say. She'd been focused on just showing up and introducing herself, not much more than that.

*Other than having the most romantic, exciting night of your life with a man you've been dreaming about for months?*

Yeah, okay, that, too. But only way down deep in the most secretive recesses of her mind. Really, the main point had been to say hello, see if he called her a big, fat, lying imposter, and then wing it from there.

So far, so good. He was smiling, and there had been definite interest—attraction—in his expression for the first few seconds. At least, she *thought* that's what it had been. Of course, then there was the fact that he didn't seem to want to let go of her hand.

But she needed to take baby steps, to see if they made it through dinner before she dared dream that she might actually have a chance of physical interaction with this impossibly gorgeous man. Later, after the hors d'oeuvres, she'd think about a kiss. And if they made it through the salad, she'd contemplate his hands touching her in very sensitive places. With the surf and turf might come images of him surfing her turf.

As for actual intercourse? God, that was so far off her radar, she didn't know what she'd even say if he suggested it. The very thought of it would just have to wait until after some kind of decadent chocolate desert. Or at least a few drinks.

Speaking of which, she wished she'd stopped in the bar and had one. It might have steadied her nerves...not to mention her ankles, which wobbled in Mindy's borrowed, ridiculously high-heeled black shoes.

"I'm just glad you didn't stand me up," he said.

"Only a crazy woman would do that," she retorted.

Though he looked curious, he didn't question her vehemence. "Well, I have to admit, I was getting a little nervous," he said, sounding laid-back and friendly, though he continued to study her face closely. The gold flecks in his green eyes twinkled, and his sexy mouth bore the faintest hint of a smile. "I know a boring fundraiser isn't the ideal scenario for a first date, but I am glad I won't have to go in there alone."

First date. Not just blind date. The term jarred her...but also gave her hope. It was one thing to contemplate having a wildly romantic adventure on a one-time-only date. But he'd said *first*...implying there could be a second, or possibly more than that. She hadn't even allowed herself to go there in her head.

Was there a chance things might not begin and end tonight? Well, maybe. Everything depended on how well they hit it off and, of course, whether he was the forgiving sort. And if he had a sense of humor.

*Oh, yeah, funny story, you see, my best friend, who's kind of easy, thought it would be a great idea for us both to lie to you, our client, and have me pretend to be somebody else for the night. Hilarious, huh?*

The chances of him laughing, too, were pretty slim. Which just made enjoying every second she had with him all the more critical. Sarah had one shot, and she intended to make this a night she would never forget. She wanted to imprint every moment on her memories, to never forget that she had, just once, stepped out of her comfort zone and gone after a lovely moment with her own Prince Charming.

As for how far this went, how intimate those moments got? Well, that was still a big question mark at the end of the fairy tale.

Sarah had very little experience with physical intimacy, but what she lacked in experience, she hoped she would make up for in enthusiasm. And while she wasn't the most beautiful woman here, she knew her body had to be sending signals. Nature itself should be telling him she was attracted to him. There was a chemical reaction between them—she felt it, recognized it, even though she'd never experienced it before.

"I do have to say, I'm surprised," he said, finally releasing her hand, which he'd held on to for at least an hour. Or a minute. Same difference when it came to this man. "You're not the type of woman I'd have expected Rick to set me up with."

Rick. Rick who? Oh, God, she was so dead. What had she been thinking? There were so many details she hadn't thought through.

"Oh, wait. You've never actually met him, right? He'd said you were a friend of a friend."

Relieved, she nodded. "Right." *Just don't ask which friend.*

"Well, you're most definitely a pleasant surprise."

"Thanks," she managed to say, clearing her throat a little. Hoping to distract him, she added, "I'm glad you're not disappointed."

"Far from it," he said, still studying her intently. She felt the heat of that stare, not to mention the warmth of his tall, firm body, so perfectly clad in an impeccable blue suit.

He was, without a doubt, the handsomest man in the building. She'd spent a good five minutes eyeing him from across the ornate lobby, trying to work up the nerve to go through with this. During that time, she'd done some people-watching.

The hotel was bursting with travelers. There were couples here on Valentine's weekend getaways, pale, northern families with kids and au pair in tow, as well as a bunch of professional types who were heading toward a ballroom for what appeared to be a large, private function.

None of them were anywhere near as attractive as he was. With his dark-blond hair, sparkling green eyes, square jaw, broad shoulders, strong chest and the rest of that tall, lean form, he drew the eye of every female, from nine to ninety-nine, who walked past him. And for this night, this one amazing, *stolen* night, he was hers.

She tried to feel bad about stealing it. But to give herself credit, it wasn't really a theft, more like...a gift.

Actually, when it came right down to it, she was just

being a good citizen and recycling. Some other woman had thrown him away, and she'd picked him up.

*Just like a Dumpster-diver. So classy.*

"I hope you'll forgive me," he said, watching her closely. "But I've forgotten your name. This came about so quickly."

The word *Sarah* came to her lips, but she bit it back with a hard chomp on her tongue, and froze. Deer-in-headlights time.

If she gave him her real name, and he later remembered, she was doomed.

If she gave him the one he was expecting, and later forgot to answer to it, she was doomed.

Face it. She was doomed.

What on earth had she been thinking? She couldn't do this. She was *so* not a seductress. She'd only had sex with one other guy in her entire life—and, just like in that movie about the forty-year-old virgin, the longer she'd gone without, the more sure she was that she just didn't have the knack for it. Seduction, sex, romance, any of that stuff. She might have a sultry voice, and she might be pretty, but some sexy cell had been left out of her anatomy. She just didn't have what it took to *make* something happen with a man.

Coming here tonight had taken every bit of courage she had. And there were so many ways she could ruin this. Not the least of which was that she had to try to keep her voice as clear and un-throaty as possible, on the off chance he might remember the operator he'd spoken with once every week or two for the past six months. All these extra little details were bound to trip her up!

"Cat got your tongue?"

"Umm…." She seriously thought about just spilling her guts. She could tell him what had happened, throw herself on his mercy. Then, if he took it well, she could ask if he'd like her to continue as his date. The worst he could do was say no.

*No, it isn't the worst he could do, he could fire you.*

Not just fire her, but say a word or two to other doctors in the area. Blackballing really wasn't that uncommon in her business. Not that he seemed the type, of course. In fact, she couldn't imagine him being so vengeful.

But the business wasn't hers, alone. Mindy was her partner, and she deserved to be protected. Sarah was already taking an outrageous risk here. She needed to do whatever she could to keep Mindy out of it.

And honestly, of those two evils—him turning her down, or him firing her—Sarah couldn't say which was worse. Losing his contract, or losing her one chance to get close to him—either one was too depressing to contemplate.

He snapped his fingers. "Oh, wait, Bambi, isn't it?"

It seemed the decision had been taken out of her hands, at least for right now. Her throat painfully tight, Sarah swallowed her conscience. In a nod so quick and tiny it could have been mistaken for a reflexive hiccup, she confirmed the lie.

"Is that a nickname for something? Or your real name?"

Feeling like she was being thrown a lifeline, she breathed a sigh of relief at being able to tell him at least one truth.

"My real name's Sarah."

"That's better," he admitted, smiling down at her. "Sorry to say, you don't look much like a Bambi. Did you love the movie as a kid or something?"

She wrinkled her nose. "No way."

*Dummy.* She should have said yes. How else was she going to explain having the nickname Bambi?

"Not a fan, huh?"

"Well, I liked the first half when I was five. That was all

I was allowed to watch of it. I never saw the ending until I was in high school."

He grinned. "Let me guess. Overprotective parents?"

"You have no idea," she said, hearing the dryness in her tone. "I had to get a friend to show me how it ended during a sleepover. Believe me, nothing brings down a sweet sixteen party like a wimpy teenager crying off the two pounds of mascara she'd put on during the obligatory makeover session."

He chuckled, that same warm, masculine sound that had given her shivers through the phone. Now, in person, it made her legs wobble. Which made the stupid shoes wobble, too. If he actually laughed, she might pitch right off her shoes into the fountain like some high-dive performer off a pier.

*So what? A handsome doctor will be right there to give you mouth-to-mouth resuscitation.*

Huh-uh. When she pictured his mouth on hers, it was with both of them in a private, secluded place. And dry.

Well, mostly dry. Her panties had been moist since this afternoon when she'd first thought about spending a romantic evening with him.

"I never liked it, either," he admitted. "So, it was just one of those weird things that stick, huh? I get that. One of my aunts still calls me E.T. Apparently I looked like an extraterrestrial at birth."

"Well, you definitely grew out of that phase."

"Yeah, I'm glad the wrinkles, purplish skin and baldness didn't last past the age of twelve or so."

With every word he spoke, Sarah felt herself relax. Every sentence reinforced the impressions she'd had of him on the phone—he was incredibly easy to talk to. He had no pretensions, he went out of his way to put the person he was speaking with at ease. Just a really all-around nice guy, at least so far.

Again she had to wonder why on earth someone like Steve Wilshire needed a blind date. He should be able to stick his finger out his car window as he drove down the street, point to any woman of legal age, and name the time and place. *You. My bed. Tonight.*

*Yes, indeed, you betcha!*

"Listen," he said, "the official banquet doesn't start for another hour. Want to go into the bar so we can get to know each other a little beforehand?"

"What is this banquet?" she asked, before realizing that perhaps Bambi already knew. Duh. If she kept this up, she'd be exposed as a phony before they even ordered drinks.

He nodded toward the ballroom entrance. "It's a physicians' fundraiser. Good cause, but pretty boring."

Yikes, a physicians' event? Mingling with the medical set was risky. She had worked with a lot of the local doctors from Jacksonville down to St. Augustine for the past few years. Some she'd even met face-to-face.

If she was going to get busted, she'd prefer to do it with a drink or two under her belt. "Bar. Definitely."

Nodding, he put a hand on her elbow, lightly, like a gentleman. But the contact sizzled. Just as it had when he'd shaken her hand. She couldn't form a thought, much less a word as he steered her toward a dark, shadowy bar. Few people were in it, probably because it was too late for the afternooners and too early for the before-dinner crowd.

Gesturing toward a small, private table in a corner, he led her to it, holding out her chair as she sat down. "Okay?"

"Fine."

They ordered drinks from a flirty waitress who smiled a little too intimately at Steve. Sarah gave the other woman a hard look. It had taken everything she had to work up the nerve to do this—going out and trying to get something she really wanted didn't come easy to her. Especially when, this time, she was going after a magical night with a special man. So damned if some poacher was going to get involved this far into the game.

They remained silent until the waitress returned. When Sarah spied her big, minty mojito, she said, "Thanks," then stuck a straw in it and sipped deeply. She wasn't much of a drinker, but tonight she needed some liquid fortification. The drink was a strong one, the rum burning her throat and the mint tickling her nose. She knew she should slow down so the alcohol wouldn't go to her head, but she couldn't help taking one more deep sip.

"Nervous?" he asked, eyeing her over the rim of his glass.

She licked her lips. "A little. I've never done this."

He hid a smile behind his drink. "Been in a bar? Don't tell me your parents have never let you have a drink, either."

She rolled her eyes. "They'd probably prefer that. But, believe it or not, I did manage to escape from under their Bambi-hating thumbs."

"Gotta give them credit, they were right about that one."

"Yes. But, unfortunately, they still wanted to protect me from the big bad dangers of the world even after I grew up. Thank God they eventually retired and moved to North Carolina."

"That's a switch," he said, "given the snowbird population around here."

"I'm not looking a gift horse—or in this case, three gift states between me and them—in the mouth."

"Let me guess. Only child?"

"Uh-huh. You?"

"One of six."

She whistled. "And where do you fall in the mix?"

"Middle."

"Ooh, so you were the troublemaker, were you?"

A wry grin answered that question. "Maybe a little."

No wonder he knew how to deal with people, how to get along so well with others. Sarah had always imagined what it would be like to have a big family, a house filled with siblings. Sadly, she suspected it was her own childhood health issues that had prevented that from ever happening. Her parents hadn't been willing to let lightning strike twice.

"Uh, back to your original question, I meant I've never done this." She waved her hand back and forth between them. "Gone on a blind date."

"Neither have I."

Unable to help it, she asked, "So why are you here?" Swallowing, she tried to make that query sound a little less intrusive. "Sorry, I mean, I'm just surprised that a handsome doctor like you needs somebody else to fix him up."

"You might be surprised. I don't meet many people outside of my profession."

"So that whole doctor/nurse thing is just an urban legend?"

"It is in my case." With a shrug, he explained, "The nurses I work with all like to talk a little too much. I feel like I'm under a microscope and they're constantly dissecting me, talking about my private life, keeping score, whispering about who I might be interested in."

"That sucks."

"Especially for someone like me, who really likes his privacy."

She understood that, and felt a momentary twinge about having invaded that privacy by coming up here tonight.

"Anyway, I meant it earlier when I said I didn't want to show up alone tonight. I'm working on a partnership deal, but I've arrived stag at one too many events to please my potential new business partner."

Ahh. The light dawned. "You don't want him to look at you and see a free-wheeling bachelor."

"Something like that."

*Then why in the name of God were you going to show up with a woman named Bambi?*

Of course, she couldn't ask the question, but she couldn't deny being very curious. It just didn't make sense that this man couldn't get his own date for any function—from a fundraiser to a have-fun-between-the-sheets-raiser.

"Speaking of jobs, you're not a nurse, are you?"

Pleased that Bambi's occupation hadn't been previously revealed—especially since the woman sounded as though she worked as a stripper—she replied, "Hardly."

Then she kicked herself for being judgmental about Bambi. The woman had been pretty inconsiderate, calling an answering service to break a date, however, there was no indication that her job involved taking her clothes off. Look at all the people who'd thought Sarah should start a 1-800 number of her own. For all she knew, Bambi could be a scientist.

Though, if she had to bet between one extreme and the other—stripper or astrophysicist—she'd lay money on girl-who-jumps-out-of-cake-at-bachelor-parties.

He lifted his drink to his mouth again, but just before he sipped, he casually murmured, "So what *do* you do?"

Oh boy. Another one of those tricky questions. If she answered truthfully, he might put two and two together and come up smelling a rat. But she'd already had her fill of lying. Such dishonesty just didn't come naturally to her. Mindy probably would have invented some grand story about being a stock-car driver or something. Sarah just wasn't wired that way—to be either a stock-car driver *or* a blatant liar.

"Wait, never mind," he said, saving her from answering. "I'd rather maintain the mystery."

Sarah stared, glad he'd made it easy for her again, but also suspicious. Her luck wasn't often this good. That was okay, usually. After the whole surviving-deadly-cancer thing as a kid, she'd figured she'd shot her wad on good luck in one fell swoop, and the rest of her life would be about hard work and dedication. Could that phantom luck really have brought her to this moment, and kept him completely in the dark about it?

Hmm. Maybe she hadn't been as successful at carrying off this scheme as she'd thought. Perhaps she'd already done or said something to give herself away, and he was just toying with her.

Which left her wondering…just who was playing who here?

And more importantly—if she still got her once-in-a-lifetime chance with Steve Wilshire, did it really matter?

# 3

THROUGHOUT THE HOUR that they sat in the bar, sipping their drinks and talking, Steve kept a mental list of possibilities to explain everything about this strange turn of events. Not the date or the chemistry, the heat, the utter attraction. Those things were a given. But the mystery of just who this woman was that he was so attracted to. That had him stumped.

He had several theories about her and why she'd pulled a switch with Bambi.

Of course, the first possibility was that she really *was* Bambi, and that the pictures on her Facebook page were phony. But he didn't think that was it. Despite her explanation, she just didn't seem the type to have that nickname— not when Sarah, soft, sweet, sexy Sarah—suited her so very well.

Plus, she was obviously nervous, and it seemed to go beyond mere first-date jitters. Though she'd relaxed— especially after sucking down most of a second cocktail— he knew she'd been ready to bolt. That was why he hadn't challenged her on things like her name and occupation.

Bambi, from what Rick had said, was a dancer. At the time, Steve had been thinking ballerina.

God, he was gullible.

The major fact that ruled out a picture-switch, however, was that Rick had *told* him his date was a tall, stacked blonde. Which had sounded fine at the time, but now seemed a little unappealing.

This woman had only one out of three of those qualities. Not that he'd call her stacked, merely beautifully curved. And he simply couldn't stop thinking about stripping her out of that dress and touching every soft inch of her.

He shifted in his seat, not wanting to dwell on that thought, not when every damn time he looked across the table at her lovely face, his eyes were drawn down the long, slender neck, the soft shoulders and that tempting swell of cleavage rising out of her satiny black dress. Frankly, he'd always been a leg man, but, oh, he was on the verge of repenting and changing his ways.

*Knock it off,* he reminded himself. *Figure this out while you still have a brain cell left.*

Okay. Back to the list.

Another possibility was that the real Bambi wasn't interested and had changed her mind. But they didn't even know each other. So why the big deception? Why not just break the date?

Another idea. Maybe this one, Sarah, was so into him she'd kidnapped his real date and substituted herself. Far-fetched, obviously. But he kind of liked the idea that Sarah had done this because she wanted to be with him...not as a favor to a friend with cold feet.

He wanted her to want him. He wanted that a lot.

Whether she did or not, there were a lot of possible explanations for what was happening here. But no definite answers. Being honest, though, he had to admit that trying to figure out who Sarah was, and how she'd come to be here, sitting across from him, all soft-skinned, moist-lipped and wide-eyed, was the most fun he'd had in months. In fact, he couldn't recall the last time he'd enjoyed a woman's company more.

Though he really needed to stop thinking about that soft skin, those moist lips and wide eyes. Man oh man, was she a distraction. He found his stare drawn again and again to a tiny scar on her throat, wanting to lean across the table and nibble on it…and proceed down her body from there. Or up. Or both.

*Definitely both.*

"Would you like another drink?" he asked.

She shook her head. "Not if it means that waitress comes around and bends over in front of you again. I swear, it's a wonder she doesn't tip over the way she sticks out her chest."

"I hadn't noticed."

"How do they let you practice medicine when you have such rotten eyesight?"

Jaw dropping, he barked a laugh, liking the slightly disgruntled Sarah. Or the slightly tipsy one…he wasn't entirely sure which best described her right now.

"You should close your mouth," she said, her eyes gleaming with wickedness. "She might trip and accidentally drop a breast into it or something."

Eyes widening, he did as she ordered and snapped his mouth shut. *Tipsy.* Given her coyness and nervousness earlier, he suspected the rum had done a little something to loosen her up.

Not that he was complaining. Not at all. She had finally relaxed, let down her guard, and he looked forward to slipping past those last walls of her defenses, to find out what had really brought her here tonight.

"Sorry," she mumbled, nibbling on her lip as if she'd just realized what she'd said.

Though amused by her bluntness, it wasn't amusement that filled his head as he considered her words. A sultry image had taken up residence in his mind. Not of the waitress, of course. No. He couldn't stop envisioning someone else's perfect breast landing in his mouth, a soft, sensitive nipple tightening beneath his tongue and lips. Oh, he wouldn't be at all averse to having his mouth on Sarah's breast…or on anything else of hers.

He wanted her. Just plain wanted her.

It wasn't merely attraction, though, of course, that throbbed and hummed like a soundtrack beneath every word they said. Beyond that, though, he liked her. She was easy to talk to, blunt, had a great laugh and a ready smile.

They'd talked about the weather and the pros and cons of winter in Florida. He loved it, having grown up in Vermont and gotten his fill of snow by age two. She hated it, having lived here all her life and romanticized those hideous blizzards.

They'd touched lightly on politics—always a risky proposition these days, but had managed to agree more than they'd disagreed. They felt the same about movies—God love a woman who dug explosions and on-screen violence. She'd revealed a little more than she'd probably wanted to about her overprotective parents, and he'd mentioned the divorce.

And all the while, he listened to her words but had a hard time thinking about much more than the delightful way her voice rolled over him, affecting him head to toe. He felt as though he could step into the warm, sultry aura it created, as though it was a physical, tangible thing between them, waiting to wrap him in a sexy embrace.

*You know that voice. You've heard it before.*

But damned if he knew where. Maybe just in his most erotic dreams.

"So, your divorce," she said, coming back to a topic they'd only skimmed. Just as he'd figured she would. "Was it amicable?"

"I think lawyers invented that word," he said wryly. "But it wasn't *War of the Roses* ugly, at least, although people probably gossiped about it almost as much." His mouth twisting, he added, "Just FYI—I really hate being gossiped about. It's one of my biggest pet peeves."

"Noted. Why'd you split up?"

"I was a workaholic, and she was a deep-sea fisherman."

Her mouth dropped open.

Steve waved a hand. "Metaphorically speaking. Actually, she was a pharmaceutical rep. Now, those are some urban legends you should believe."

"And?"

"And she was trawling for the great white. I was the tuna that got caught in her net." Remembering his ex's romantic track record, he added, "But at least I wasn't the carp she caught first. I didn't even know about him until after we'd split up."

She gasped. "She lied about having been married before?"

"She lied about a lot of things," he said with a shrug, having long since gotten over the catastrophe that had been his marriage. "From big things like marriage right down to how much she spent on shoes in a month."

Across from him, Sarah looked away, her long lashes drifting lower over her eyes as she mumbled, "A real gold digger, huh?"

"It wasn't the money," he admitted, having realized that

for himself long ago. "It was the prestige. Her first husband was a dermatologist."

"And treating heart-attack victims is a step up from helping teenagers get rid of their zits?"

Laughing, he said, "You got it."

"Let me guess...her next one will be a neurosurgeon?"

He lifted a brow and feigned offense. "You're saying neurosurgery is more prestigious than cardiology?"

"Only on *Grey's Anatomy,*" she insisted, holding her hands up in instant supplication.

"Okay, then. Yeah, you've got the gist. She remarried a couple of months ago...to a chief of staff at a big hospital down in Miami. I doubt he knows he's number three."

Rolling her eyes, she muttered, "I think the Surgeon General's wife better start watching her hubby like a hawk."

Funny how immediately she grasped the whole situation, all the while maintaining a genuine warmth. He had to add quick-witted and intuitive to the long list of things he liked about Sarah. Damned if he couldn't see himself falling for this woman, even if he didn't know who the hell she really was.

Not yet, anyway.

But the evening was still young. She'd let her guard down while engaging in light conversation. Soon enough, he'd get back around to asking the kinds of questions that might trip her up...or at least get her to drop the pretense and admit what was really going on here.

Steve didn't like to be lied to. In fact, he hated that even more than he hated being the center of gossip.

But so far, other than saying she was his date, he didn't think she'd outright lied. She'd looked relieved to give him her real name, and after that, he'd made sure not to put her in the position of having to make up anything. Every word she'd said since had had a genuine and natural ring to it. Real. Something about tonight—about Sarah—made him think that, no matter how this looked, she wasn't lying. She *wanted* to be here, with him. And she'd done something to make that happen.

He'd find out the whole story soon enough, he had no doubt. In the meantime, he was quite willing just to enjoy the mystery.

"What about you?" he asked her, after dwelling on what he could ask without making her so nervous she couldn't speak. There was one thing he wanted to know. "Ever married?"

She shook her head. "Barely dated, to be honest."

That he found hard to believe.

His skepticism must have shown itself. "I'm serious."

"Then the guys you went to high school with were blind."

"I was home-schooled. I went to community college for two years. But since I didn't have a driver's license, my father drove me."

"Your parents weren't just overprotective…"

"They were freaks," she said with a laugh. Then, as naturally as she would say *I'm a Libra,* she added, "I'm a cancer survivor."

Steve immediately frowned, watching her lift a self-conscious hand to her throat. That scar.

"My parents were crazy-overprotective, but only because I'd gone through a really rough time that lasted several years. I was diagnosed when I was nine, and it went on and off until I was a teenager."

"What kind?"

"Esophageal."

He whistled, truly surprised. The odds against a nine-year-old contracting that were huge.

"I know. It's rare."

"Incredibly."

"My mother blamed my father for having smoked a few cigars when I was a kid, and he blamed her for eating in restaurants where people smoked while she was pregnant. The fact is, sometimes things just happen." She shrugged. "It is what it is."

She was right, and the attitude wasn't an uncommon one amongst older cancer survivors. But he admired her for having realized it at such a young age. Then something else clicked.

"That explains your voice."

"Yup."

"Wow, now I feel like crap for being so turned on by it."

Instead of being offended, she looked positively delighted at his words. The sparkle in her eyes matched the pleased smile on her lovely face. "Really? You are?"

Like any red-blooded man wouldn't be? "Yeah. It's... very mysterious."

"It can be, I guess," she admitted. "I have received one or two suggestions about what kind of job I could get with it."

"What, doing narration for film or taping audio books?"

She nibbled her lip for a second, averting her eyes in embarrassment, then mumbled, "Uh...phone sex."

She was so damn cute when she said it—visibly self-conscious and embarrassed at having brought it up. Obviously, she hadn't noticed that he was already sitting over here trying to pretend he hadn't had sex on the brain since they'd touched hands out in the lobby.

"I've been told I would be a natural," she said, her cheeks pinkening even further.

A natural at sex. Oh, yeah.

Then he realized that wasn't what she'd meant. She'd meant whispering graphic, wicked things, telling a man what she wanted, how she was touching herself and how she wanted to be touched by him.

He grabbed his nearly empty glass, bringing it to his mouth to try to slurp up any last remnants of moisture left behind by the nearly melted ice. Because even talking about phone sex with this woman to whom he was already so attracted was very dangerous indeed. He needed to cool off and to occupy his mouth so he wouldn't just come right out and ask her if she wanted to blow off the fundraiser and get a room on one of the floors above them in this swanky hotel.

"The idea is pretty ridiculous," she said with a self-conscious chuckle. "Especially considering I'd have absolutely no idea what I was talking about."

Steve had just sucked a small piece of ice into his mouth. With that comment, the chunk went right down his throat, choking him for a second. He coughed into his fist.

"Are you okay?" she asked, wide-eyed and innocent.

Maybe too innocent. If that wasn't a hint of humor lurking on those lush lips, he'd be very surprised.

Rather than dance around it anymore, he came right out with what he was thinking. "Are you telling me you're a virgin?"

Clearing her throat, she gave a tiny negative shake of her head. "Not quite."

"Believe me," he said, "it's not the kind of question that can be answered with a 'kind of.' You are or you aren't."

"I can't believe I'm about to tell you this—it must be the mojitos," she said with a helpless shake of her head.

"To answer your question, technically, no, I'm not. But, uh, let's just say my first time was one away from my last…and neither one was enough to get me breathing hard, much less ready to comprehend what all the fuss is about."

He ran his fingertips over his damp glass, both stunned and incredibly turned on. Stunned because she was far too beautiful to be so inexperienced. Turned on because, oh, did he like the idea of helping her learn all she wanted to know. The chance to show this woman what all the fuss was about made that hotel room idea look better and better.

"So, even if I'd ever consider it, which I wouldn't, I'd be no good in the phone-sex game. Because I assume men who call those numbers are looking for a Baskin-Robbins sexual experience—lots and lots of flavors." She shrugged, looking unsure of herself, as if she had no idea how incredibly sexy she truly was. "They don't want *me,* who's so bland I don't know if I could even claim to be vanilla ice cream. Maybe I'm ice milk. Frozen yogurt, at most."

Steve could only stare. He'd never been so aroused at the talk of ice cream. Or any dessert. He had to shift in his chair as his trousers constricted around his rock-hard cock. Especially because he sensed Sarah was telling him these things not to engage in naughty conversation…but because she really wanted him to know. For some *specific* reason.

Suddenly, one possible reason occurred to him for her presence here tonight. Had she switched with Bambi—been so nervous and then flirtatious—because she wanted to move on down the menu from single cone to triple sundae with hot fudge and cherries on top? If so, did it make any difference whatsoever that *he'd* be the guy holding the ice cream scoop…or would *anyone* do just as well?

He didn't see how she could have been specific about

him, never having met him before. How could she? And
suddenly the idea that she would be sitting here seducing
any guy who'd happened to be standing by that fountain
in a blue suit made him a little nauseous.

*You were ready to do the same thing.*

Yeah. Maybe. He'd definitely thought about breaking his
dry spell with the woman he was being fixed up with.

But that was before he'd met Sarah. He now suspected
he wanted more than that…more than one night to blow
off steam. The only question was, did she? If he took her
upstairs now, would she be gone with the dawn, disappearing from his life as quickly as she'd entered it?

He couldn't know.

Which meant he couldn't take the risk. Not yet. Before he made love to Sarah, he intended to be very sure it
wouldn't be the first *and* the last time.

# 4

FOR THE FIRST HOUR of the banquet, Sarah spent her time studying the crowd, looking for a familiar face. She didn't see any, fortunately, but she sure saw a bunch of familiar names on table settings and in the program. Apparently a whole lot of doctors who had contracts with Call Anytime believed in this cause and had come out to support it.

Darn. If only she worked for skinflints.

Still, she didn't think it was going to be too much of a problem. Mindy handled most of the sales stuff, meeting face to face with customers. Sarah covered the books, the payroll, the business end. So she had met very few of their clients in person. And since she seldom worked the phones, she hadn't talked to many of them, either. In fact, Steve Wilshire was the only one she'd spoken with more than two or three times, and so far, he hadn't had an "Aha!" moment and unmasked her. Or, unvoiced her. Whatever.

"Doing okay?" Steve asked, an unspoken apology in his low whisper. The two of them sat with a large group, which included the doctor he was hoping to partner with. And frankly, all of them, while very nice, were so boring they could have made a kid hopped up on Red Bull and Twinkies drop for a languorous nap.

"Fine," she murmured.

"I owe you for this."

She smiled a little, liking the sound of that. "I'll hold you to it." Hmm. She liked the sound of that, too. Holding him to anything...especially herself. She'd been thinking of little else since their conversation in the bar.

Her frankness had probably taken him by surprise...but not as much as it had surprised her. She didn't know why she'd volunteered so much personal information. It could have been the two drinks, which had gone right to her head. Or it could have been the fact that he was so easy to talk to. Or just that she wanted him so much. Heck, maybe she'd been trying to proposition him in her own inexperienced, clumsy way.

Whatever the reason, the result hadn't been the two of them racing to the nearest room with a bed. As if the subject of phone sex and her inexperience had never come up, he'd simply paid for their drinks and escorted her into the banquet. He'd been the perfect gentleman. Which she found incredibly attractive, and terribly frustrating.

She'd wanted one night of romance with her dream man. Now she wanted...more. Just more.

Maybe not anything as blatant as getting laid, as Mindy had suggested. But a kiss on the cheek just wasn't going to cut it, not now that she'd shared intimate conversation with him, felt the warmth of his breath on her cheek as he sat beside her, experienced the brush of his strong hand on her skin.

*You want to make love with him. Admit it. You always have.*

It was true. Now more than ever.

"How about we get out of here early and go somewhere else for dessert?"

She sucked in a breath, feeling caught at having erotic

thoughts about him. She also wasn't sure if he was propositioning her, especially given their ice-cream conversation.

His sudden grimace said he realized that himself, and he clarified, "I meant, we could get coffee or something. It wasn't a sleazy come-on, I swear."

"Should I be relieved or offended that there was no double entendre in that invitation?" Honestly, she wasn't sure which she felt. Not that Steve was at all the cheesy/sleazy sort—he wasn't—but she wouldn't mind thinking that he had, at least, given thought to making improper, but oh, so welcome, advances.

He lifted a curious brow. "Meaning?"

She could hedge, or change the subject, but the clock was ticking. She might only have this one night with this man, and with every minute that went by, she suspected that just a romantic date wasn't going to be enough.

She had tiptoed around her attraction…maybe it was time to be a little more forward. "I mean, I think I'd be pretty sad if you were *only* interested in coffee. Not…a hot fudge sundae."

"Thirty-one flavors?" he whispered.

"With whipped cream on top," she replied, wondering where she found the courage to be so bold. She licked her lips, knowing he couldn't take his eyes off them. "And a cherry."

He didn't say anything for a minute, just stared at her. His attractive green eyes narrowed the tiniest bit, and his mouth opened as he drew long, even breaths—in and out—as if thinking of a response.

Finally, he gave her one. "I'm interested. Very interested."

He didn't say another word, letting his tone and the heated expression on his face tell her everything she needed to know. His whole body was tight and aware, from the hard leg that brushed against hers underneath the table, up to his stiff jaw. He seemed to be fighting some inner battle...mind over matter. Or, in this case, mind over sexual response.

She bit her bottom lip, thrilled that he'd confirmed it. He wanted her. This handsome, sexy man who'd begun seducing her on the phone months ago without even knowing it, wanted her in his bed.

She felt like laughing, she felt like running. She felt like dancing, like hiding under the table. She wanted to slide over onto his lap, straddle him, twine her fingers in that thick hair and taste every inch of him. She wanted to apologize for being a bald-faced liar.

She wanted...him. Just him.

But they were surrounded by people—his colleagues—in a public place. So the tension that had been building in her for months, ever since their first conversation, couldn't be released. The steam just had to keep on building. She hoped her head wouldn't blow off before they finally had some time alone..

Or before he found out she was a fake and ditched her.

No. She couldn't think that way. This was going so well. They'd shared laughter and easy conversation. Absolutely the only thing wrong with this whole situation was that she wasn't the woman he had been expecting tonight.

*So just make sure you are the woman he wants tomorrow.*

The elderly woman sitting on Steve's other side suddenly asked him something, and he turned to address her. Sarah took the opportunity to grab her glass of water, taking a few long sips to try to tame her racing heart. Not to mention her raging libido.

She had barely set the glass back down when she realized she was being spoken to. "So, Sarah, what do you do for a living?" asked Dr. Tate, the cardiologist Steve was hoping would go into partnership with him. He seemed like a nice man—if a little dull. But his wife had been very friendly, and appeared very happy to see Steve walk in with a woman on his arm. Right now, though, she wished they were a little less friendly—and less apt to ask questions.

Seeing Steve still engaged in conversation with the older woman, she replied as truthfully as she could. "I'm in communications."

That was not a lie. She was more into communications than anybody here. You couldn't get something much more communicable than telephone work.

*Communicable.* Sounded sordid. Then again, to this very proper doctor and his wife, stealing somebody else's blind date probably was a little sordid.

*Steve said he's happy you're here.* And he'd sounded as though he'd meant it, so she really needed to try to let go of the guilt, at least long enough to see if there could be something more between them than one single date—or one amazing, perfect night in each other's arms. That anything more could only come after a moment of reckoning was something she didn't want to think about right now.

"And how did you and Steve meet?"

Not knowing how to answer that, since she wasn't sure how much Steve would want revealed, she was relieved when he jumped into the conversation. "Mutual friends," he said simply, dropping a light hand on Sarah's leg beneath the table.

She knew it was meant to be a reassuring it's-our-secret kind of contact. After their previous conversation, though, after he'd admitted he wanted her, she couldn't possibly take it as sweet and innocent. Regardless of how that warm, firm touch was meant, the reality was pure, sizzling excitement. Hearing his quick, surprised inhalation, she knew he felt the same way.

It wasn't as though he was touching her in a terribly intimate area—his hand was much closer to her knee than to anything that could be called the money-spot. But the strength of that hand, the possessiveness, the warmth…it took a simple touch up a notch into wicked intimacy.

His fingers were strong, hot against the bare skin of her thigh. He had a man's hands—not too smooth, just right, in fact. That, combined with the dessert-and-phone-sex conversation, had them both hyper aware of every look, word and, definitely, of every touch.

"Let's dance," he suddenly said in a low voice. He didn't so much ask as order, as if he, too, needed to get away from the table and probing eyes. Whatever their conversations had been, however pleasantly the evening had been going, things had just gotten a whole lot more personal. All because of a silly conversation about coffee versus dessert and a simple touch.

Heaven only knew what was going to happen when the touches became less simple. But oh, complications had never sounded so appealing.

Nodding wordlessly, she let him take her hand and help her up. He squeezed lightly, saying without words that he knew it had just gotten about ten degrees hotter in the room, but said nothing as they wove through the tables to the small dance floor. A band playing what she'd normally call old-people music stood on a small stage. By unspoken agreement, they moved past the other couples, heading for a far corner, near the door leading to the kitchens.

Then he stopped, turned and took her into his arms.

Sarah didn't even realize she'd been holding her breath until it slid out of her in a long, slow sigh at the feel of his tall body pressed against hers. Though she'd been cursing the high heels all evening, she couldn't deny that they helped everything line up very nicely. His trousered legs brushed against her bare ones and his hard chest pressed against her breasts, bringing their tips to rigid attention.

She had heard of people melting into someone else's arms, but had never really experienced it…until now. Her whole body went soft, accommodating all his hardness. Angles sinking into curves, two disparate forms conjoining into one.

"Mmm," she said, closing her eyes.

He made a similar sound, then rubbed his cheek against her hair. "Has this ever happened to you before?"

She didn't pretend to misunderstand. "No."

"I mean, we barely know each other."

That was true, even if she did know him a little better than he knew her. Still, she had the feeling that even if this had been a real blind date and she'd never heard his voice, never seen his picture, never half fallen for the calm, warm way he talked about his concern for his patients, she'd still be drawn to him the way she was right now.

"You just feel right. This feels right," she whispered.

He held her a little tighter, if that was possible. Sensing the ridge of heat pressed against her lower tummy, she knew he was losing the battle to keep control.

"All you have to do is open your mouth and I start to get hard," he admitted.

Rather than shocking her, his honesty thrilled her. Steve was bringing out the hidden side of her, the flirty, sensual woman who'd been repressed by her illnesses, her inexperience, her family situation, her job and her own insecurities. It was that side that responded. "You have some ideas about what you want me to do with my mouth?"

He groaned, his hands dropping lower so his fingertips

brushed the top curves of her bottom. Light, delicate strokes made her arch closer. Not really paying attention to anyone around them, she didn't even notice they were moving off the dance floor until she felt the hard laminate beneath her heels give way to softer carpeting. Quickly glancing around, she realized they'd ended up behind the raised platform where the band was performing, and were, in fact, hidden from view by both the stage and all the equipment on it.

Steve didn't have to tell her why he'd pulled her out of sight. Instead, he showed her. Without a word, he bent and covered her lips with his in a hot kiss. Sarah groaned in her throat, tilting her head and parting her lips, inviting him to explore deeper. He did, his warm tongue sliding into her mouth to meet hers in a slow, sultry mating.

They didn't stop dancing—or at least swaying. Their bodies were pressed together so closely not a sound could have passed between them. And the kiss went on and on, all the warm, spicy flavors of this man filling her up, sustaining her, arousing her to a fever pitch. Her nerve endings came alive, each strand of hair, every inch of skin. The connection was utterly electric and she felt it right to her core.

Finally, seeming loathe to do it, he ended the kiss, brushing his lips against hers one last time, then pulling away. He didn't go far; his jaw brushed her face and she could hear, by his shallow breaths, that he was every bit as excited as she.

"Nice," he finally murmured.

"Very."

Suddenly, against her stomach, she felt something thrum. "My God, it even vibrates?" she said, jerking her head back.

Steve let out a low laugh, then shook his head apologetically. "I'm sorry. It's hard to escape being on call when you're in a solo practice."

On call. The answering service. *Oh, God.*

"To be honest, I thought if tonight went really badly, I could have the service page me with a drummed-up emergency."

She raised a querying brow. "And now?"

"Now I really wish I'd gotten someone to cover for me."

So did she, and not only because she hated the thought of them being interrupted. The last thing she wanted was for Steve to start thinking about the answering service—and about one particular whiskey-voiced operator who sometimes relayed his messages.

Nibbling her lip, she watched him step farther away from the stage—out of earshot of the band—to check his pager. With an apologetic shrug, he then used his cell phone to call a number Sarah knew by heart.

It probably *was* an emergency, of course. Doctors had them all the time, and he wasn't the first to receive a page at the fundraiser tonight. Heck, he probably wasn't even the first to receive a page from Call Anytime.

Still, a tiny suspicion blossomed in her mind that Mindy could be meddling. Sarah had intentionally left her cell phone turned off so her friend could not call to see how the date was going. She wouldn't put it past the other woman to make up some call in order to get Steve on the line…to find out whether he was still out or had already called it a night.

Huh. If she had her way, he wouldn't be calling it a night until tomorrow morning.

Having kissed him, been held by him, Sarah was more sure than ever that she wanted to go to bed with Steve Wilshire. She wanted it desperately. Especially given how very much he seemed to want her, too. They had just clicked, the way she'd always suspected they would. The only thing standing in their way was the issue of the secret blind-date swap-out.

*So tell him the truth.*

She would. Soon. The few words he'd said about his wife—*the liar*—had rung loudly in her ears. Sarah hated liars, too, and God knew she didn't want to be one. Something deep inside just wouldn't allow her to go through with the entire plan—to steal one amazing, romantic night with him under false pretenses. Especially if that night ended up with the two of them in bed together.

Yes, he knew her real name, he'd spent an evening with the real woman; however, he needed to know the whole truth. And before they went any further, he would. In fact, she was going to tell him the very moment he returned.

Only, judging by the concerned look on his face after he finished his call, she might not have her chance.

"I'm so sorry," he said as he tucked the phone back into his suit pocket. "I have to go to the hospital. There's a serious problem with one of my patients."

Her shoulders sank in disappointment.

"Believe me, I'm not happy about it, either," he told her. "I had envisioned tonight ending a lot differently."

"I understand," she said. "Another time."

There was an emergency. She had to believe that, and didn't want to read any more into it.

*You can ask anybody at the service if he'd called in and asked them to page him.*

That was the inexperienced, unconfident Sarah's voice whispering doubts in her brain. It was that same Sarah who feared that if he said, *Sure, I'll call you sometime,* she'd probably curl up in a ball and die. She couldn't stand the thought of having misjudged him—them—so badly.

Too caught up in her own dark imaginings even to look in his face for the truth, she turned to leave their sheltered spot. But his hand on her arm stopped her. "Meet me for dinner tomorrow night."

Her jaw dropped open and her heart sang. "Seriously?"

"Absolutely." Grinning, he added, "Admit it, for a second, you thought that was a made-up emergency call, didn't you?"

She bit her bottom lip, not answering.

Rolling his eyes, he put a hand on her shoulder. "I *do* want to see you again, tomorrow night. There's a place a couple of miles up the beach, called Jolly Roger's. You can't miss it."

She knew the place. The name made it sound gaudy or touristy, but in truth it was a small, intimate seafood place loved by the locals. Sitting on a private stretch of beach, its views were beautiful and she couldn't think of a better spot to get things out in the open between them than on a lovely patio overlooking the churning waves.

"This isn't good-night." He lifted a hand to her face, tracing his fingertips across her cheek, then twining them in her hair. "It's just a twenty-one-hour break. Then we start over again. Seven o'clock tomorrow night."

Start over. As much as it pained her to stop now, with her mouth still tingling from his amazing kiss, she knew it was the right thing to do. Tomorrow would be the perfect time to come clean, to admit who she really was and how tonight had really come to be. Then they could start fresh. Besides, what was twenty-one hours when she'd been waiting for her chance with him for so long?

"Okay," she told him. "Tomorrow night it is."

# 5

By 6 p.m. on Sunday, Steve was beginning to worry.

By 6:45 p.m., to sweat.

And by 7:00 p.m., he was just about in panic mode. Because he was still at the hospital.

He was going to be late for his dinner date. Very late. And fool that he was, he hadn't gotten Sarah's number, so he couldn't call to tell her that. Hell, he hadn't even learned her last name!

He'd tried calling the restaurant only to be put on hold on the reservations line for what seemed like hours. In the middle of a crisis, he'd handed the phone to a nurse, begging her to relay the message. Then *she'd* been kept on hold and had to get back to work, too. So the message was never passed on.

"Damn it all," he muttered as he finally pulled off his scrubs and got dressed in the hospital locker room. He considered swinging by his house to change. It was only a half mile from the restaurant, one reason he'd suggested it. But he didn't want to waste even that much time. So he settled for wearing the khakis and golf shirt he'd put on before coming in this afternoon to check on the patient who'd gone critical last night in the middle of his date.

The patient was doing much better, and Steve should have easily been able to get home in time to get ready. But then an emergency case had come in. A seventy-year-old had keeled over on the golf course—yeah, like that was something different, here in The Sunshine State. Steve had been brought in to consult and it was seven-twenty by the time he flew out of the hospital entrance and hurried to his car.

Tugging his phone out of his pocket, he tried the restaurant again and, this time, when they tried to put him on hold immediately after answering, he wouldn't allow it. "No! Do *not* put me on hold, I've been trying to get through for an hour."

"Sorry, sir, but we're very busy," a young woman said, talking loudly to be heard over voices and the clank of dishes in the background.

"I'm meeting a woman there and I'm running late. I just need you to tell her I'm coming."

"Sure, sure, I'll tell her."

"Don't you want her name?" he bit out, getting annoyed.

She said something to someone else, then yelled, then finally responded, "Okay, sure, what's her name?"

"Sarah."

"Sarah what?"

"Uh, just Sarah. She's petite, gold-streaked brown hair just past her shoulders. Beautiful."

He heard the woman's sigh.

"Please, just try, would you?"

She hung up without even answering. Steve could only hope Sarah had enough faith in the hours they'd spent together last night to know he wouldn't stand her up.

*Why would she? She barely knows you?*

Not a comforting thought.

But at least she knew his last name. She'd called him by it last night. It was possible she'd gotten worried, looked him up and tried calling him. She wouldn't be able to get his unlisted home number or his cell, of course, but she could have tried the office and gotten the answering service.

The answering service that was directing all his calls— on his express, very firm orders—to Dr. Tate tonight. Steve had gotten the other doctor to cover for him, wanting to make sure he and Sarah had one uninterrupted evening together. He hoped it wouldn't be for nothing.

*Be there, please be there,* he thought as he headed down the coast. But when he got to the restaurant ten minutes later, frantically looking at every person and every table, inside as well as out on the deck, he knew she wasn't.

He strode to the hostess station. "I called a little while ago to leave a message for my date. Sarah."

The woman's mouth opened in surprise "Oh!" The hint of apology in her face told him all he'd needed to know, but she said it, anyway. "I'm so sorry, but we were slammed. It's Valentine's weekend. I just forgot." She came out from behind the counter. "I'll help you find her."

"She's gone," he said flatly, angry, though mainly at himself for not making sure he knew how to reach Sarah. He wasn't usually so careless. But he'd been off his game, off balance since the minute he'd laid eyes on her. "It's too late."

Shaking his head and thrusting a frustrated hand through his hair, he walked outside. There had to be a way to fix this. Racking his brain, he tried to think of possible ways to get in touch with her. He had the Facebook page book-marked, but considering it hadn't really been hers, he didn't expect that it would do him much good. And Rick probably wouldn't be of much use, either.

His mystery woman might just remain a mystery forever. He might never see her again.

Feeling his head pound at the very thought, he reached his car, on the edge of the parking lot right beside a wooden staircase leading down to the beach. A strong gusty breeze blew sand and grit in his face, and he blinked, rubbing at his eyes. When he opened them again, something down near the water caught his attention.

A slight figure in a filmy, light-colored dress was moving along the shore, walking in the cold winter surf. The bright stars and nearly full moon overhead made her visible, but not recognizable. Still, something inside his optimistic heart wondered if it could be Sarah. Disappointed at having been stood up, might she have decided to go for a night walk on the beach?

Not giving it a second thought, he jogged down the steps onto the sand and walked toward her. "Sarah?"

She stopped, turned around. And as he drew closer, he realized Fate had been very kind to him tonight.

"I am so sorry!" he said, closing the distance between them in a few long strides. He stopped about two feet away, seeing the way she nibbled on her bottom lip. Her eyes were suspiciously bright. "I had an emergency at the hospital and had no way to reach you. I don't even know your last name."

She studied him, as if gauging his sincerity, then murmured, "Did the restaurant's phone not work?"

He quickly explained, hoping she would believe him.

Her mouth might have softened a tiny bit, but her tone didn't. "Are you sure you just didn't have second thoughts? I mean, we barely know each other. If you didn't want to see me again…"

"I did." He reached out and put a hand on her shoulder. "Look, if I intended to stand you up, why would I have come at all?" Taking the chance that she'd want him to, he moved even closer. "I wanted more than anything to see you again. I've thought about nothing else since last night."

She sniffed, then mumbled, "Bet your patient wouldn't be happy to hear that."

Smiling gently, he said, "I'll make it up to you, I promise." Tugging her even closer, he saw the indecision flash across her face. She was angry, still not quite trusting him, but wanting to believe. He saw that, and he understood it.

"I'm not used to this, Steve," she finally admitted. "It's all new to me, and I don't like how I felt, sitting there at that table, being stared at, pitied. I don't like feeling so vulnerable."

His heart twisted. "I'm so sorry," he repeated, picturing her waiting, her spirits crumbling. Every sweep of the minute hand must have convinced her she'd been stood up, and that she should never have trusted him to begin with. Sarah had laid out her inexperience last night; he knew she couldn't have a lot of self-confidence. He'd give anything to take that uncomfortable episode back. "Please forgive me and let me make it up to you."

Resisting for one more moment, she finally let him draw her into his arms. She wrapped hers around his waist, melting against him. They stood silently for a long moment, then, in a prim voice, she said, "I already ate."

"Even dessert?"

She tensed the slightest bit, then tilted her head back and looked up at him, those amazing eyes glittering in the moonlight.

They both knew what kind of dessert he was talking about. He wanted to dine on her, feast on her, have her in every way a man could have a woman. He wanted to pleasure her, show her what *"all the fuss was about."* Wanted to show her how sorry he was that he'd made her doubt him—made her doubt *them*.

And he wanted to do it right now.

Out here, on the beach, with the breeze whipping against their bodies and the sound of the surf churning, everything felt so much more…elemental. Primal. Including what he felt about her.

He just couldn't wait anymore, he was dying to taste her. Dipping his head, he caught her mouth and kissed her deeply. He plunged his tongue against hers, hoping to show her that he wanted to be here, wanted her, wanted *this*.

Reaching up, she twined her arms around his neck, not resisting when he lifted her, holding her tightly against him. When her slim legs rose and encircled his hips, he groaned out loud. Her filmy dress did nothing to conceal the womanly heat between those perfect thighs, and he reflexively ground his rock-hard erection against her.

When the kiss finally ended, he didn't let her down. Instead, glancing over his shoulder at the restaurant not too far behind them, then at the next structure down the beach, he said, "My house is right over there."

Her eyes widened. "Really?"

"Uh-huh. Call me overconfident, but I was hoping we'd end up there after dinner."

"You could have just invited me to your house to begin with," she whispered, leaning closer to nibble on his earlobe. "We could have started with dessert."

"Does that mean I'm forgiven?"

"You're definitely off to a good start."

Her fingers were twined in his hair, her soft breaths brushing over his skin. He felt encompassed by her, and so on fire he wasn't sure they would make it to his place.

But it wasn't as if they had much choice. Anybody could walk down from the parking lot.

"So, it's okay with you if we go to my house? Because I want you, Sarah. I want you badly," he said, making sure she knew what she was really saying yes to.

She didn't even hesitate. "Get me there now, or I'll get us both arrested for public indecency."

HER CAR WAS UP in the parking lot, and she suspected Steve's was, too. But when he said it would be faster just to walk up the beach, Sarah believed him.

Not that he let her walk. Not one step. As if she weighed nothing, he carried her, kissing her, stroking her, heightening her need to a fever pitch with every step he took across the sand. Sarah kept her legs around his waist and her arms around his neck, holding on to his big, strong body, knowing he would not let her fall.

Though she didn't think she'd soon forget how awful she had felt sitting at that table, surrounded by couples celebrating the romantic holiday one night early, she wouldn't trade the end result for anything. She was going to have a night of sensual pleasure with her fantasy man. It would be all she'd ever dreamed of, and more than she'd ever hoped to have.

*You deserve this. You both deserve this.*

She wasn't the same quiet, shy girl she'd been during her younger years. Now she was a woman, a desperately aroused woman. No more second-guessing herself. She wanted nothing more than to give and receive pleasure, to share erotic intimacy with the man holding her so strongly in his arms.

Needing to taste him, she slid her tongue down his neck, sampling a rippling cord of muscle. She nibbled lightly on the spot where neck met strong, powerful shoulder, and felt him shudder against her. He was rock-hard between her thighs, and every step rocked him harder where she most needed rocking. By the time they'd reached a wooden crossover leading up to his beachfront house, she was quivering, on the verge of something wonderful. Something she'd only ever experienced with the vibrator she'd bought when she'd first moved into her own place.

"Oh, please," she whimpered, feeling waves of sensation rise in her body as steadily as the waves were hitting the shore.

He kissed her again, deeply. He'd been holding her bottom while he walked, and now shifted one arm a little, so he could slide his other hand into far more intimate territory. She hissed at the feel of those strong fingers on her inner thigh, close to the elastic edge of her panties. Close, but not close enough. "More."

He obliged, stroking her, until his fingers moved under the filmy fabric to tangle in her soft curls.

Sarah groaned, gasped and quivered. And when that gentle, questing touch found the throbbing center of all sensation, she gave herself over to a consciousness-altering orgasm.

"Oh, my God!" she cried, throwing her head back to look up at the sky. She jerked, rubbing against him, wanting more. More pressure, more pleasure, more of everything. And the waves just kept coming like the steady, reliable tide. Over. And over.

Finally, when she could think again, she realized they'd actually made it up onto what must be his back patio. Steve didn't even try for the door, he simply walked over to a plush chaise longue and dropped her onto it. Arching and curving as the last effects of pleasure reverberated through her, she watched him strip off his shirt, then unfasten his trousers.

His chest was rippled with muscle, his body lean and strong, like a runner's. She lost her breath, unable to think about anything else except how those hips would feel between her bare thighs.

"You're beautiful," he mumbled, staring down at her.

Sarah didn't even hesitate, she simply began to pull her dress up, inch by inch, revealing to his eyes what he'd already experienced with his hands. Seeing him grab the back of a chair for support gave her so much confidence that she was smiling seductively by the time she drew the dress up and off.

She wore nothing but the panties underneath.

"Beautiful," he repeated before dropping to his knees beside her.

He ran one hand up her bare thigh, catching the panties with his fingertip, then drew them down. Now wearing absolutely nothing, she lay still, like a kid in that ice cream shop, not knowing what flavor she wanted to try, just sure vanilla would never cut it.

"Are you cold?" he asked, stroking his palm up and down her side.

"Not one bit." No, she was burning up, in fact. Everywhere he touched, a tiny ember erupted into flames, igniting every one of her senses.

He began to caress her, stroking her stomach, her hips, her thighs. Those big hands were capable of infinite tenderness and the barely-there touches soon had her writhing on the chaise. They were wonderful, but she wanted more. A lot more.

"Please," she cried, arching toward him, thrusting her chest up invitingly.

As if he'd merely been waiting for the invitation, he instantly moved his mouth to her breast, catching her nipple between his warm lips and sucking deeply. She felt the pull clear down to her toes and sighed happily, twining her fingers in her hair. He went back and forth, giving equal attention, using his fingers to tweak each sensitive nipple when his mouth was busy with the other.

Soon her hips were jerking reflexively, lifting, seeking the ultimate pleasure she knew he could give her. But there was one more pleasure she hadn't been prepared for. And when he finally moved his mouth away from her breasts and tasted his way down to her body, right to the curls of her sex, she let out another wavering cry.

"You taste so good," he muttered against her mound as his tongue tasted her clit.

Sarah had never experienced that particular intimacy, and she almost flew off the chaise. But that would mean he'd have to stop. And oh, God, she did not want him to stop.

He settled in, clearly with no intention of stopping, sucking her sensitive nub into his mouth, tasting, kissing. When his hand moved to tug at her thighs, she let them fall open to him, exposing herself fully. Steve moved his fingers up, testing the slick folds of her body. Carefully, gently, he slid one finger into her wet channel, going slowly, doubling the delight he continued to offer with his mouth.

Another orgasm swept through her. She began to shake, helpless against her body's response. Pleasure gushed through her, shocking at first, then slow and steady.

"You take my breath away," he told her once she'd finally floated back to earth.

While she'd been lost to bliss, he'd stood up, and finished unfastening his pants. Sarah watched with hungry eyes, desperate to see him, more desperate to have him—all of him. "Mmm," she groaned.

"You getting what all the fuss was about?" he teased. She nodded.

"No more vanilla?"

"I think I'm ready for the chunky monkey."

He said nothing else, just pushed his pants and boxer briefs down, revealing a thick, jutting erection. Every part of her that wasn't already dripping with want melted, and she parted her thighs farther, desperate to have him between them.

Before he knelt, though, he tore open a condom he must have had tucked in his pocket. God, she hadn't even thought of it. Some smart, contemporary woman she was.

Lifting her arms, she pulled him down to her. "Now."

"Now," he agreed as he began to ease into her, carefully.

She knew he was going slowly, treating her like the near-virgin he knew she was. But she didn't want restraint. She wanted the passion, the utter intensity that was making all his muscles bunch up, his face redden and the cords of muscle in his neck throb.

Reaching down, she grabbed his hips, arching toward him, trying to take what he wasn't giving. "More," she begged.

He resisted for a half second, then, with a groan, he plunged deep and hard, filling her completely.

This time it wasn't just a cry, it was a scream of pure pleasure that erupted from her lips. She probably startled the night birds winging over the water. Steve covered her mouth with his to swallow her joyful noises with a kiss.

They began to move, to sway, giving and taking, pulling and thrusting. Everything fell into place, as if they'd been made to do this with each other. Every stroke was answered, every offer of enjoyment accepted and reciprocated.

It lasted a long time. At one point, they shifted positions, so he was the one lying on the chaise and she sat on top of him. Her feet braced on the cool patio, she was able to ride him. Taking what she wanted, she drove him wild, judging by the look in his eyes as he stared up at her.

Finally, he grabbed her hips and held her tightly against himself, groaning as he finally climaxed. And then he pulled her down onto his chest, holding her tightly in his arms as the world gradually returned to focus.

"You okay?" he asked her, several minutes later, when it felt as though both their heart rates had returned to some semblance of normalcy.

"I am more fine than I have ever been in my life."

She meant that.

"I can't tell you how grateful I am for blind dates."

She couldn't help stiffening a tiny bit. God, with everything that had gone on tonight—from thinking he'd stood her up until they'd made wild, crazy love on his patio—she'd forgotten all about what had brought them together.

Her lies.

"I mean, talk about luck," he continued. "Who would have thought something this good could come out of a set-up?"

She swallowed, wanting to tell him. Needing to tell him. But unsure how to find the words. Naked and entwined also equaled vulnerable.

"How rare is it for two adults to find each other without having to play a lot of games or pretend to be people they're not just to find out if they're compatible?"

Playing games. Just as she'd been doing.

Steve traced a hand along her spine, sliding his palm down over her bottom. "I haven't felt this good in a long time. I wasn't sure I would ever be able to trust a woman again, but you, Sarah…well, I trusted you the minute I saw you."

"I felt the same way, from the first time I heard your voice," she whispered, meaning that.

He kissed her again, interrupting anything else she might have said. Then he sat up, carefully disentangling them and asked, "How about we take this inside?"

"Good idea." Inside. Clothed. In the light. Maybe then she could tell him how this whole thing had happened... and then see if he still thought blind dates were such a good thing.

Moving languorously, they pulled on their clothes, and she watched as he unlocked the back door. Once inside the house, she took a moment to look around, marveling at the beautiful place.

His house wasn't huge, certainly not a mansion—though, for a beachfront property, he'd probably paid as much as an inland mansion would have cost. All decorated in soft blues and yellows, the house seemed a perfect complement to the sun-drenched blue sky he probably saw out of these back windows every single morning.

"Drink?"

"Just water. I worked up a thirst."

"Ditto." He walked over to a wet bar area, opened a small refrigerator and pulled out two bottles. "Have I told you yet how glad I am that you went for that walk? I mean, I was getting desperate, trying to figure out how to reach you."

She liked the sound of that. She'd been feeling pretty desperate herself tonight. "Desperate, huh?"

"Yeah. Like I said, no last name, no phone number, I didn't know where you work, where you live. Nothing."

Which was exactly what she'd wanted. To think it had almost cost her this amazing, unforgettable night.

"Since I knew you knew *my* last name, I was hoping you'd try to reach me on my work number, which is published. I thought about calling the answering service to see if a sexy-voiced stranger had called and asked about me."

She tensed again as he handed her the bottle. "I didn't."

"Just as well," he told her. "Believe me, I did *not* want to call in there and give a bunch of lonely-hearts operators more reason to gossip about my private life than they already do."

Lonely hearts? That's what he thought of the women who took his calls—of her? She couldn't help stiffening a little. "You think they talk about you?"

Opening his water bottle, he dropped onto the couch beside her. "Of course they do. Everyone seems to, lately. I told you about the nurses. My own staff started giving me advice during the divorce." Sighing deeply, he continued. "And my *loving* ex had a habit of intentionally calling my work number when she knew I was unreachable. She'd leave messages with the answering service to cover where she really was and what she was doing."

Oh. Sarah began to get the picture. His ex-wife was not the only one who tried to use Call Anytime as an alibi. Cheating professionals actually did it all the time. Her anger rose as she realized that's probably what had been happening to Steve.

"Believe me, it's not pleasant to realize complete strangers are privy to your innermost secrets. You hire them to do a job and they end up holding your entire private life in their hands."

She swallowed, licking her lips, looking at it from his perspective. Sarah trusted her employees, and privacy issues were stressed as highly as efficiency. Yet she'd been the one to break those rules more than anyone else.

"I had to switch companies after the divorce because I was so damned humiliated when one of them started asking me if I was dating again yet. Another one told me I was better off without her."

Oh, God. She closed her eyes, feeling sick.

He didn't appear to notice. "I felt, I dunno...violated. Personal calls and messages going through complete strangers, knowing they were whispering about me the minute I hung up the phone, that was one thing. But people I'd never met speculating about my wife running around on me, and then feeling free to comment on it? Not my idea of fun."

Feeling dizzy, Sarah gulped her water. She was having a hard time focusing. Though at first, she'd been offended at being called a "lonely-hearts operator," she had opened up her ears enough to hear what Steve was really saying. To hear the tone in his voice—the embarrassment a proud, private man had felt. The humiliation. The hurt.

His wife must have been one piece of work. He didn't sound as if he was still wounded by having lost her, but rather by how it had thrown open his personal life to the world. While very friendly, he was obviously a person who liked to protect his privacy, and he'd been helpless to do it.

His trust had been violated...by her, most of all. She hadn't just eavesdropped on his private life, she'd inserted herself into it.

The magnitude of what she'd done last night really began to hit home. It wasn't just about lying anymore. There was no explaining this away as a little fib or a prank—*and oh, look how well it turned out, so let's just forget about it!* They were way past that because she'd done exactly what those others had done during his ugly divorce—she'd gotten involved in his private business, involving herself when she had absolutely no right to do so.

She could never forgive herself for being so selfish, so thoughtless. So how could she expect him to forgive her?

Feeling trapped, she eyed the back door through which

they'd come, and the front one on the far side of the house. There was no easy way out of here. No explanation he would accept. She couldn't possibly pretend she wanted to leave, not now that they'd proven in the most elemental way possible just how perfect they could be together. Nor could she get away without telling him her last name and phone number.

"Done?" he asked her, taking the empty water bottle from her hand.

Before she could say anything, not that she knew what she'd say, he reached for her hand and pulled her to her feet. "Outside was amazing. Now I want you somewhere a little more comfortable."

She hesitated, knowing it was wrong, knowing she had no business sleeping with him again under these pretenses. But she also knew he wasn't going to let her go.

*Besides, this is your last chance to be with him.*

That sad little bit of truth made her want to cry. But it was true. This was her last moment with the man of her dreams—the man she knew she could easily fall in love with. One last night before she disappeared out of his life as quickly and mysteriously as she'd entered it.

So, rather than making some excuse and leaving, she reached up, cupped his cheek, and whispered, "Then take me to your bed."

# 6

SHE WAS GONE.

Awakening at dawn, and rolling over to pull Sarah into his arms, Steve had been shocked to find nothing but an empty bed. The rumpled pillows, tangled sheets and a strand of silky hair were the only evidence that she'd been there.

Blinking, he sat up, immediately glancing toward the bathroom, even though the silence in the house—the emptiness—told him he wouldn't see her there. Nor did he think she was in the kitchen making coffee or something. The air was just too still. There wasn't the clink of a spoon, or even a whisper of sound above the inevitable churning of the waves outside.

"What the hell?" he muttered, getting out of bed to prowl the house, just to be sure.

Nothing.

Last night had been amazing. *Everything* had been amazing since the minute they'd met. So why would she just leave without waking him? It made no sense. If she had to go to work or be somewhere, she could have told him.

Then he groaned, remembering something else. "You don't even know where she works, jackass."

Nor did he know her last name. Even after almost missing her at the restaurant, he'd *still* neglected to get that basic bit of information. Or her phone number.

About to smack himself in the head for being so stupid, he suddenly spied a sheet of paper on his kitchen table.

*Thank God.* She'd left a note, probably to explain her departure and tell him how to reach her. But as he picked it up and read, he realized it wasn't what he expected to hear.

Dear Steve,
Please forgive me for skulking out of the house before you woke up. The truth is, I just can't face you. I've been lying to you. I'm not Bambi, I never was. I "stole" Saturday night's date with you…substituted myself in her place, all because I was selfish and wanted a chance with you.

I know you hate liars, and you hate having your privacy invaded, and I've done both. Hearing you talk about it last night broke my heart and made me feel like the worst person alive. I hope you can forgive me someday. Sarah.

He stared at the paper for a long time, then let it fall from his fingers to flutter back to the table, thinking about every word he'd said, every bit of conversation.

Yeah. He'd talked about those things, but not because he was trying to make her feel bad or coerce any kind of confession. The only time he'd been trying to do that was after they'd made love on the patio, and he'd told her how grateful he was for blind dates! He'd said it intentionally, opening the door to let her come clean about how she'd really come to be his date Saturday night. When she hadn't walked through that door, he'd figured she just wasn't ready yet. But with their intimacy and connection growing with every passing hour, he knew she would be soon enough.

He'd never—not once—equated her with his ex. Sarah wasn't a liar, and he'd never considered her to be one. Nor did he get the whole invading-his-privacy thing.

Yet, thinking about his words, he began to see how she would think he'd hate her for lying.

What a mess.

But one that he could fix. Because he wasn't willing to let her go, not without making sure she knew he wasn't angry that she'd "stolen" such a magnificent, wonderful weekend with him. He hoped like hell she'd want to keep seeing him afterward, but at the very least, she deserved to know he wasn't angry…and he deserved to hear her whole story.

"How?" he muttered. How was he supposed to find her?

He wondered about it as he made coffee, then showered and got ready for work. He was still wondering about it in his office later that morning, between appointments and friendly conversations with his staff, who were busily chattering about their Valentine's Day plans.

Just his luck. He found someone he'd like to spend the romantic holiday with…and he didn't even know her last name.

Finally realizing he did have at least one thing to go on, he tracked down Rick. Not wanting to get into the whole story, he merely asked his buddy to see if he could get in touch with Bambi—the real Bambi—to find out what had happened Saturday night. Why she'd backed out, and who might have known about it.

His friend called him back a half hour later. "Dude, Bambi's on the road, on her way to Texas. She met some other guy and took off. I'm really sorry, man. I had no idea she was gonna bail on ya."

"It's okay," he said. "What did she say about it? Did she send one of her friends in her place?"

*"Huh?* Somebody else showed up?" His friend was silent for a moment, then chortled. "Oh, I get it! And you want to know how to get a hold of her."

"Yeah, Captain Obvious, I do. So what exactly did Bambi say?"

"She didn't mention anything about swapping with some other chick," Rick admitted, sounding sorry to deliver bad news. "She said she was in such a rush to get out of town, she just called your answering service and asked them to tell you she wasn't gonna be there."

Steve quickly thought back to Saturday afternoon, remembering the message from the service about his date. But that didn't make sense, either. When he'd called in for the message, they'd made no mention about his date not showing up.

"Okay," he said, sighing with disappointment. "Thanks for checking it out."

"Let me know what happens. It's about time you get your membership back in the sexually-active club."

He was back in that club. Now he just wanted to get his membership card and *stay* there for a while. With Sarah as his club-mate.

Hanging up, Steve sat at his desk, the thoughts continuing to churn. Something was nagging at the back of his brain.

Some woman—not Bambi—had called the answering service, pretending to be her in order to get the information about the date. But, if that was the case, what had happened with Bambi's original message? He'd never gotten it.

The service. The answer had to lie there.

Reaching for his phone, he buzzed his office manager. "Would you bring me the information on the new answering service company we hired a few months ago?" he asked, still trying to figure it out. It wasn't that he needed the message retrieval number; he called it all the time and knew it by heart. But somehow, he didn't think he'd get the answers he wanted by dialing it now.

Then he thought of all those calls. Dialing that number. Getting his messages. And he remembered something else.

A voice.

"Son of a bitch," he whispered, everything starting to click into place in his brain.

"Everything okay, doctor?" asked his office manager, who'd just walked in carrying a few sheets of paper.

"I'm fine," he told her, shaking his head in disbelief.

"Okay, then, here's the info you wanted," she said, leaving the pages on his desk before walking out. He barely even noticed.

Was it possible? Could the whiskey-voiced operator he'd talked to on the phone several times while retrieving his messages *also* be the whiskey-voiced seductress he'd spent the past two evenings with?

It sounded crazy. But it also made perfect sense. And when he glanced at the papers on his desk, including a pamphlet for the company—Call Anytime—he knew it was the truth. Because right there in black and white were the names of the owners.

One of whom was Sarah Holt.

He'd found his mystery woman, knew who she was and how she'd come to meet him Saturday night. Thinking about everything he'd said last night, he also now completely understood why she'd walked out on him this morning.

Now he just needed to figure out what he was going to do about it.

"YOU ARE AN INSANE PERSON."

Trying to ignore her friend and partner, Sarah hunched deeper into her chair, wishing she'd never spilled her guts to Mindy about what had happened this weekend.

She should have just called in sick. Pulling the covers over her head and ignoring the world would have been a much better way to spend Valentine's Day. Having to come in to the office and listen to all her employees coo about their boyfriends and husbands, or, even worse, open the door to receive boxed roses or candy, was just plain painful when you had a broken heart.

Hers shouldn't be broken. She'd only gone out with the guy twice. Still, she'd known Steve Wilshire was something special before she'd set eyes on him. And those two evenings had been the most wonderful ones of her entire life. To think she would never get to sleep in his arms again, as she had last night, had her ready to burst into tears. Just like she had the minute she'd gotten back to her place in the pre-dawn hours this morning after sneaking out on him like a thief in the night.

"I mean, you tell me you're crazy about the guy, that you hit it off, that you actually spent the night with him last night…and then you just left?" Mindy was stalking around the room, railing, drawing the eyes of every operator on the floor. Considering the office she shared with Mindy was like a fishbowl, with glass walls, they had zero privacy. Everyone was paying attention, making no effort to hide it. "How could you do that? That is so not what nice-girl Sarah does!"

"Nice-girl Sarah doesn't lie her way into a guy's bed, either," Sarah snapped, sick and tired of hearing about stupid nice-girl Sarah. "I told you how he feels about liars, and about people who invade his privacy. Weren't you listening?"

"But none of that matters if he really cares about you. And it sounds like he could!"

They were going around in circles. The two of them had been having this same argument for a couple of hours, ever since this afternoon when Sarah had finally broken down and confessed why she was so miserable.

"Look," Sarah at last admitted. "He called operators lonely hearts and griped about them being nosy."

Mindy's mouth tightened. She took that personally.

"He can't stand liars, people who don't mind their own business…and answering-service operators. I am batting zero for three here, don't you get it? If he ever finds out the truth, he's liable not only to tell me off, but to fire us!"

Mindy opened her mouth to argue a little more, but Sarah put a weary hand up. "Would you just let it go? It's over. I took my shot, did what you wanted me to, had sex with my dream man and now I'm moving on."

Mindy glared, her mouth twisting in a frown. Throwing herself down in her chair, she said, "That's not what I wanted and you know it. That's what *I* would do. Not you. You're too nice for that. And you deserve to be in love."

"I think I *am* in love," Sarah replied sadly, touched as she finally realized Mindy's anger was generated by true concern for her.

"Oh, honey. I'm so sorry," Mindy whispered.

Yeah. So was Sarah.

Before she could say anything further, though, she saw Mindy's eyes grow wide. Her friend was facing the wall, while Sarah's back was to it, and something had obviously happened in the busy answering area.

"Stay here," Mindy snapped, leaping out of her chair.

Sarah began to turn around, but Mindy demanded, "No. Don't move. Just stay put. Let me see what's going on."

Then she hurried out of the office, slamming the door shut behind her.

There must be some drama happening with the operators, apparently. It wouldn't be the first time. Everybody's emotions ran a little high on holidays like this one. In a 24-hour-a-day, 365-days-a-year business, somebody always got stuck working when they didn't want to. So an employee who hadn't gotten the night off had probably said something snarky to someone who had.

Then she heard a man's voice, and Sarah's curiosity grew. They'd had a couple of male operators in the past, but none lately. Before she could get up to see what was happening, she heard Mindy respond to someone. Shockingly, her voice was raised, her tone angry.

"No, you're not going to talk to her until you tell me you're not here to give her a hard time. It was all my fault. If you want to blame somebody, blame me. You can even fire us, if you want. But don't take it out on Sarah."

Suddenly having a suspicion, Sarah leapt up and swung around. Staring through the glass, she saw Steve Wilshire. He stood in the middle of the bullpen, surrounded by operators, blocked from moving by a belligerent—protective—Mindy.

Their eyes met, hers, she knew, round and shocked, his...inscrutable.

Sarah's heart raced, her blood roaring as she understood the ramifications. He'd found her. Which meant he'd been looking for her. The only question was—had he come here to tell her off, and to fire her, as she'd told Mindy she feared? Or for some other reason?

Steve wasn't paying any attention to Mindy, or to anyone else. It was as if nobody other than Sarah even existed at that moment. His stare never wavered from her face.

Then he smiled that slow, tender smile, saying a million things without uttering a word.

"Oh, God," she whispered.

Her heart lifted, and a sense that everything was going to be okay washed over her, making her feel so hopeful, so happy, she didn't even recognize herself as the same woman she'd been an hour ago.

Still silent, Steve moved his arm, which had been behind his back, and lifted what he'd been hiding. A dozen roses. Beautiful, rich, crimson roses.

Mindy, finally noticing the flowers, not to mention the fact that Steve and Sarah couldn't take their eyes off each other, melted out of the way. Fierce mama lion protecting her cub—it was cute. Now, though, she and everyone else understood what Sarah had the moment she'd seen that smile.

He'd come here because he forgave her and wanted to be with her.

Still too surprised even to move, Sarah simply waited as Steve walked across the bullpen, skirting work-stations staffed by open-mouthed, wide-eyed women. When he got to her office and opened the door, she spared a moment to wonder woefully what her hair must look like and how red and swollen her eyes must be. But the warm, appreciative expression on his face as he stared at her said he honestly didn't care.

Entering, he pushed the door shut behind him, then took one step toward her.

She took a step, too. Then paused, saying what most needed to be said. "I'm sorry."

He lifted a hand to her face, brushing her hair back, then tangling his fingers in a few long strands. Pulling her closer, he whispered, "I'm not," then gently kissed her.

Sarah wrapped her arms around his neck, losing herself

to his embrace, somehow already knowing she would never—ever—tire of being in his arms. She kissed him back, again and again, silently repeating her apology with every soft, tender brush of their mouths.

Outside the office, there might have been some *oohs* and *aahs,* and she definitely heard clapping. But Sarah ignored everything else except the warmth of his body pressed against hers. She drank her own happiness from his lips, drowning in the tenderness of his hand on her face. And, most of all, the realization that he was here.

He'd come for her—knowing who she was, and what she must have done. And he still wanted her anyway.

The string of soft kisses finally ended, and Steve lifted the roses, offering them to her. "So, what do you say Sarah *Holt?* Will you be my Valentine?"

She nibbled her lip, wondering what on earth he'd gone through to figure out who she was. She looked forward to hearing the story…after she got finished showing him how very glad she was that he'd done it.

But that was all for later. Now, there was only this man, that smile, that amazing kiss. In his arms, she found everything she'd ever wanted and fantasized about.

Only, it was more than that. Because the reality was so much better than any dream could ever have been. She'd wanted one night of fantasy with her secret Prince Charming, but now suspected she'd landed in the most important relationship of her life with a sexy, wonderful man. A man looking at her with want and devotion in his eyes.

She'd never get tired of that look. Not ever.

"Well?" he asked.

"Yes, Steve Wilshire," she assured him, meaning it with all her heart. "I would love to be your Valentine."

\* \* \* \* \*

# EX MARKS THE SPOT
## Jo Leigh

To Brenda: You've been in my corner from the start, and I appreciate that so much.

# 1

As much as Paige Callahan loved living in San Francisco, which was a lot, there were nights when climbing the hill to her apartment was a pain. Thing was, there was no convenient street parking, so there was inevitably a search that began with hope and crossed fingers, and always ended with her trudging up block after steep block, arms loaded with briefcase and tote, until she finally made it inside the building, where she then had to climb two sets of stairs.

Normally, the view from her living-room window made her feel instantly better, but not tonight. She dropped her stuff on the dining-room table, though she wanted to throw it across the room, and considered pouring a glass of wine. Too much trouble. Instead, she listened to her phone messages, surprised that there was more than one.

"Paige, I've left this message on your cell, sent you an email and now I'm resorting to the land line. We're still on for tonight, right? The restaurant is to die for, and I swear you'll love the club. It's been forever since you've been out dancing, and I know we can find the right number of drinks that'll make even you feel like shakin' your groove thang. I know you're going to meet someone fabulous tonight, I mean it. You know I'm psychic when it comes to hot guys, and, honey, tonight is your night! Seriously. Call me or face my wrath."

"Fiona," Paige muttered, as she deleted the message, "your wrath is a cupcake with sprinkles compared to the rest of my week. My *groove thang* is broken beyond repair."

The deal she'd been working on for six months had fallen apart today. As the senior director of major gifts for the San Francisco Museum of Modern Art, Paige was responsible for obtaining pieces for exhibit. The bigger the prize, the more complex the transaction, and this one, an outright gift of four Kandinsky major works, would have been a spectacular coup.

She'd poured her heart into this deal, only to have the donor decide at the eleventh hour that he'd rather give the paintings to his grandchildren who had no interest in donating or lending.

All this on a Saturday, her day off. A miserable, freezing February twelfth, which was supposed to have been spent hanging out with Fiona and Shelly at the day spa, followed by a long-awaited dinner at the Slanted Door. She'd even agreed to go dancing at Club 525, despite the fact that she really didn't care for the DJ scene. The only reason she'd said yes was because it had been a really long time since she'd met anyone even halfway decent, let alone someone she actually wanted to sleep with. But right now, all she wanted to do was crawl into her bathtub and stay there until the whole apartment complex ran out of hot water.

After a piteous sigh, Paige pressed the button for the next message.

"Don't hang up."

Paige stilled, her breath caught in her throat, instantly recognizing Curt, her ex-boyfriend. Curt, who hadn't called her in over a year, and that was only to accuse her of stealing his CDs, his portable DVD player and his Red Sox T-shirt. She reached for the delete button, but not quickly enough.

"I know you don't want to talk to me, and I don't blame you. I've been a…less than my best. Anyway, this isn't a joke or a trick and I swear to God I have no ulterior motives. I went to this gallery showing last night, and I ran into this guy I know from Berkeley. He's a good guy, divorced, has his own tech business, and he's got a significant private art collection, right up your alley. We had some drinks, got to talking. Long story short, I gave him your number. I know, I should have asked first, but I think you two might…"

There was a long pause, and Paige could picture Curt clearly. Sitting in his uber-expensive chair, his computer monitor cluttered with his stock tickers, accounts, sports scores. He'd be clicking away on his mouse, constitution-ally incapable of talking on the phone without checking his email.

"Anyway, his name is Noah. You can tell him to screw off if you want to, but I think…"

Curt cleared his throat. "Paige, I wouldn't have given him your number if I didn't think you'd be safe. He needs a date for Monday night, for a fundraiser at a gallery, and he's also interested in lending some of his modern-art col-lection, but I bet you could get him to donate some, too. Major pieces. And, um, I found the CDs. And the DVD player, and well, turns out I left the T-shirt at the gym. So, sorry about all that, but hey, maybe this thing will work out with you and Noah and we'll be square, huh?"

She heard the ding of his email alert.

"Okay. I hope this isn't too crazy. We should, you know, talk some time."

Paige's finger still hovered over the delete button, but

she didn't press it. What she did do was collapse on the couch.

Curt was setting her up on a blind date. Curt, her boyfriend for two years, who would have been *the one* if it hadn't been for his pathological need to manipulate everything and everyone in his life. *Curt* was setting her up on a blind date for Monday night. February fourteenth. Valentine's Day. Great.

And no, she and Curt wouldn't be square, even if Noah donated a damn wing to the museum. Okay, that would make her a lot less angry, but still. A setup by Curt. A setup she needed desperately, now that six months of work had gone down the drain. It was humiliating. Tragically pathetic. Especially because she was going to say yes.

SHIT, HE'D FORGOTTEN TO CALL the museum woman. Noah Hastings checked his watch, already knowing it was too late. She'd have been asleep for hours, and what the hell was he still doing up at three-thirty in the morning? That was the trouble with internet work, it was always there, hovering. A particularly vicious hack targeting online bank passwords had been detected, and his staff at White Hat Resources was working around the clock to stop it.

Noah had gathered a group of the best hackers in the world to his company, and it seemed as if none of his team ever slept as they held disaster at bay for banks, corporations and government institutions.

Noah trusted his people, but that didn't mean he could sit back and relax. He was one hell of a hacker himself, and this particular job presented an almost irresistible challenge. On the other hand, he wasn't just a hacker any longer and he had to sleep, eat regular meals, oversee and delegate. It was nights like this, hacks like these, that made him miss his lone-wolf days when he went mano a mano with some of the smartest bastards on the planet.

He stood, stretched his neck, his back. Turned off the parts of his computer system he could. His footsteps echoed as he crossed his dark living room, the lights of the city obscuring the stars. He forced himself to think of other things as he headed upstairs to bed. One glance at the print of an early Arshile Gorky painting that hung in the hallway and he forgot everything except his plan to protect his private collection of abstract expressionist art. It still stung that his ex-wife had gotten the original in the divorce.

He had no real desire to go to the fundraiser at the Channing Gallery, but at least meeting Paige Callahan would kill two birds. He'd be seen supporting the arts, and he'd find out everything he could about the benefits of setting up a private foundation versus outright museum donations.

Actually, inviting Callahan would kill three of those metaphorical birds. It also gave him an excellent Valentine's Day date. One who had no expectations, who cared nothing about the fact that his divorce was now final and that he was technically once again on the market. He most definitely was not. One divorce was all he was willing to experience. Monday night would be strictly business.

OF COURSE, PAIGE THOUGHT. Why wouldn't Noah call during the fifteen minutes she'd been away from her apartment? Why would Curt give the man her cell-phone number, even though he knew she was twice as likely to be with her cell than at home? She had no business saying yes to this date. Meeting. Interview thing. Not the way her luck was running.

She looked back at her phone. She still didn't know Noah's last name, and it hadn't shown up on her caller ID. But his number had, so she called him back. After four rings, she got his voice mail. Again no name, just his number.

"It's Paige Callahan from the museum. Sorry I missed your call. Try me on my cell, I've got that with me all the time." She gave him her phone number slowly, twice.

An hour later, he called back when she was in the bathroom, without her phone. After cursing her horrible luck and worse timing, she listened to his message.

"Damn, I thought we'd… I hate to do this, but I'm going to be hard to reach before tomorrow evening. Instead of playing phone tag, perhaps we can meet at the gallery? I'm normally not this informal, but work is problematic at the moment. Leave a message for me, either way, and I'll completely understand if the arrangement doesn't work for you."

That was it. Naturally, she called him right back, and naturally, it went directly to voice mail. "Paige again. I'll meet you at the Channing at seven. I'm looking forward to it."

As she disconnected, all the energy, which wasn't a lot, drained out of her. She still had no idea who the mysterious Noah was, what he looked like, or if he even had a collection worth thinking about. She'd called Curt to ask. Curt hadn't picked up or called her back, which was just the sort of thing Curt would do, confirming that she couldn't take anything that might happen at the gallery for granted. It would have been easier to cancel, but the fundraiser at the Channing was a very big expensive deal, and even if Noah turned out to be in cahoots with Curt, there would be other collectors, legitimate collectors, she could meet.

She listened one more time to Noah's message. He had a good voice. Deep. Sexy. He sounded tall, nice-looking. But who was she kidding? He could look like a hunchbacked troll, it wouldn't matter. This wasn't a date.

NOAH WASN'T FOND OF wearing a tux, although since White Hat Resources had taken off he'd collected four of the damn things. There was always some formal dinner, some gala, some fundraiser that required his attendance. He wasn't fond of those, either. But his company represented security and stability, and therefore he had to represent the same things to his clients.

Tonight's event was peppered with clients and potential clients, although he'd have to do some tap-dancing with personnel if he took on much more work. Great hackers weren't easy to find, and he didn't want to risk burning out his most valuable people.

He looked at his watch again. It was still far too early for the museum woman to have arrived. His arrival at six had been a favor to Leon, the gallery's owner, who was having trouble with his computer. It had nothing to do with hacking, which Noah had known beforehand, just some operating-system errors. He'd fixed things in ten minutes and had spent the next twenty looking at the auction pieces. There were two he'd liked from very promising young artists. He headed back to look at them again. Before he made a bid, he wanted to be sure.

# 2

SHE SHOULD HAVE TAKEN her car.

Paige stood in the middle of Timmons Street, watching as her favorite—her only—shawl disappeared around the corner. Carried away by the wind, aided by her tripping over her own feet, the shawl was currently stuck on the bumper of a Muni bus, being taken to places unknown, where it would most likely have a much better evening than she would.

It was freezing. Windy. Rain was imminent. She had to walk up a big honking hill and then another three blocks to get to a street frequented by cabs. Meaning her feet would hurt all night.

She should just go home. Go home, get out of the dress that had cost her a week's pay, put on her flannel pajamas and have herself a good cry. It was all going to be a disaster anyway. Valentine's Day. What idiot thought up that bit of torture? Sure, Curt had done a few nice things in the past, but before Curt, hell, during Curt, this so-called holiday had been as romantic as a vacuum cleaner.

As she started up the hill, resigned to her fate, she counted off just a few of the wonderful February four-teenths she'd had: She'd been stood up. Three different times by three different guys. Abandoned at a concert. In San Jose. Without enough money to get home. That had been a real treat. Oh, then there was the night her date, a Stanford man studying particle physics, had been violently sick all over her brand-new silk shirt. Sweet.

She should have just worn her damn coat. Her goosebumps had goosebumps and her teeth had started to chatter. She rubbed her bare arms, as if that would help.

If only the Kandinskys had come through. She'd never have agreed to go to this fundraiser. She'd have found out exactly who her ex had set her up with, do proper research first. She'd get recommendations, find out why, if he had major pieces, she hadn't heard of him.

Watch, this Noah character would turn out to be an international art thief who would bilk the museum out of millions. Yeah, that sounded about right.

The wind blew her hair into her face, and it was all she could do not to break down and bawl like a baby.

AT TEN AFTER SEVEN, Paige shivered as she shut the taxi door. She'd made it to the gallery, late but in one piece, for whatever good that would do. But she was here, so she might as well go inside. She squared her freezing shoulders and walked toward her fate.

The hostess of the Channing, Anna, whom Paige had met at quite a few fundraisers just like this, expected her, had known she was meeting Noah. The older woman informed Paige that his last name was Hastings and gave her an odd grin as she pointed Paige in the right direction.

"Oh," Paige whispered with a tiny gasp. He most definitely did not look like a hunchbacked troll.

Anna chuckled. "Have a wonderful evening."

"Well, things are certainly looking up," Paige murmured as she reminded herself that the night might feel romantic with the gorgeous art displays, the scent of the fantastic floral arrangements and champagne at her fingertips, but she wasn't here for canoodling, or even thinking of canoodling.

NOAH HAD ALWAYS DISLIKED mixing art with business. Art was his solace, his refuge. Music, too, but paintings, from famous works to street tags, if they hit him the right way, lingered, soothed and freed up the parts of his mind too concerned with computer code. His best ideas had sprung fully formed after indulging in his passion, losing himself in an artist's vision.

He glanced at his watch yet again. She was late. His gaze went to the gallery entrance. People were gathered near the door itself, so it was conceivable that she was already here. He had asked the hostess to send the woman his way, but perhaps Ms. Callahan hadn't spoken to Anna.

Curt hadn't described Callahan, not the physical part. He'd said she was smart, told him about her degrees and her work in restoration and authentication. That she was young to be as good as she was.

Noah knew Curt and Paige had been a couple, but no longer were. It hadn't seemed acrimonious, not from Curt's tone or from the fact that he'd offered her number. Noah hadn't asked any questions, not about the two of them. It hadn't seemed relevant. Now, though, he wished he'd looked up more than her museum biography.

A waiter came by with champagne, which Noah declined, and when he looked up again, a pretty woman stood at the front entrance. From her posture he knew she was searching for someone. He wanted it to be him.

The thought made him frown. The woman at the door was attractive, yes, but from a distance. He had no idea about the details and frankly, the details had always mattered to him more than the whole. But he was also a normal man and his brain often skittered to *want* when he saw *pretty,* usually for a second or two, then something else would catch his attention, or if he was in the mood and it seemed feasible, he'd make his move.

This reaction hadn't been a momentary blip, but a four-count beat, heavy on the resonance.

There was no real reason to think the beautiful blonde was Paige Callahan. In fact, the woman now standing next to the hostess was a more likely candidate with her laptop-sized bag and her nice but sensible dress.

His gaze moved back to the beauty. She wore bangs, her hair looked tousled and sexy. Her skin was pale and her face lovely. He moved toward the door, and she came more into focus with each step. Her dress wasn't the least bit sensible. The blue was the color of a Monet sky and it flowed around her curves like liquid.

Closer still, he saw the blue might just match the color of her eyes.

She smiled his way, raised her hand in a quirky little wave.

*Let her be the one,* he thought. It would make the whole evening so much more pleasant.


So, HE WAS GORGEOUS. Tall. Filled his tuxedo exquisitely. Tonight was all about the business of art, the part that had zero sex appeal. She had to woo him, all right, but for paintings. Donations. Lots of donations. But first, they had to meet.

"Paige?"

She nodded. She appreciated the fact that he extended his hand instead of going for an air kiss or, God forbid, a hug. She hated to do that with strangers, even men with chiseled jaws and great cheekbones. "Mr. Hastings."

"Noah," he said. Instead of the shake and release Paige expected, he held her hand in his, not moving, not squeezing, just…holding. "I'm sorry to do this to you tonight of all nights. Curt assured me it wasn't going to be a problem, but now that I see you, I imagine there are a lot of broken-hearted men in San Francisco this evening."

She felt herself blush, would have pushed her hair back if she'd had both hands free. "No, it's my pleasure. Actually, I would have been watching Netflix movies and eating microwave popcorn. This is much better."

He smiled. Nicely.

It hit her, what she'd said to him, and she died just a little bit. Microwave popcorn and chick flicks. She might as well have told him she wore granny panties under her flannel nightgown.

He looked down at their joined hands. His dark eyebrows rose as if he hadn't realized, and then he let her go. "What do you say we go get something to drink before we wander through the gallery?"

"Sounds excellent."

He touched the back of her right arm as he accompanied her to the main showroom. His hand was warm and it sparked a chain reaction that made her lose her step. Which made his grip tighten. Even though she'd caught herself before disaster struck, she knew her chest, her neck and most especially her cheeks were flushed, which was inappropriate and inconvenient as this wasn't the time or the place, and for heaven's sake, she was twenty-seven, not sixteen.

There was no way Noah hadn't seen her blush, but she hoped he attributed it to her clumsiness.

"Have you been to this fundraiser before?"

"Yes," she said, grateful for something to focus on besides the fact that his hold on her arm hadn't loosened at all. "The year before last. They raised over a million-five at the silent auction. I'm a big fan of supporting the arts, especially when so much of the money goes to education and preservation." She fought off a wince. Of course he knew all that.

"According to your biography, you were in preservation for what, two years?"

"That's right. Not at MoMA, though. At the Ryerson Museum in Santa Clara."

"I've never been there."

"Too late now. They've closed. Their collection is spread out all over the world."

"That's happening too frequently," Noah said. "Yet another reason for meeting you tonight. I want to share the pieces I have, and will have, but I don't want to put them at risk. From what I've learned, you know a lot about that."

"I do. I know we can come up with a plan that will be perfectly tailored to your needs."

He guided her gently toward a standing bar and they got into line behind a couple they both knew. He was a big shot at Skywalker Ranch, the George Lucas film facilities, and his wife was on the board of the Asian Art Museum.

Paige had known she would run into a great many acquaintances and colleagues, and that this was just the start of the socializing portion of the evening. She wondered again why she hadn't heard of Noah Hastings before tonight. If he had a substantial collection, it should have been on her radar. The only thing she could think of was that he'd just started collecting.

Drinks were finally secured, and she and Noah even scored some wonderful but small hors d'oeuvres before they began the tour of the exhibit pieces, all of which were up for auction. This particular fundraiser focused on the current art scene. Up for bid were pieces from the finest new artists from around the world. The buyers were willing to spend money based on their belief that this artist or that would end up being a superstar. In fact, for some lucky painters or sculptors, tonight's outcome could be the turning point in their careers.

"I'm curious," Paige said, hoping that if they kept moving they wouldn't be interrupted, because finally, *finally,* she felt herself. This was her world, after all, more important than a man whose touch could cause her to trip. "What brought you to collecting?"

Noah paused in front of a Georg Baselitz canvas. "Five years ago I was working on a project in Chicago, stopping a cyber threat attacking the stock exchange. I didn't have my current staff then, it was mostly just me and two other guys. I was thinking in circles, had to clear my head. I ended up at the Art Institute, and I got lost in a painting by de Kooning. I stared at it for a couple of hours and then I had it. The fix."

When Paige looked up, it was to find Noah looking at her, not the painting. He had blue eyes, but they were nothing like her own. His were the color of the sea and they were somehow disarming. She felt studied, but it wasn't uncomfortable. He should look closely. He needed to trust her.

Of course, she studied him right back, and it was in the small lines around his eyes, around his mouth, that she discovered more of him. Her first impression had been of a serious man, yet the history of his laughter was right there on his face. She guessed his age in his early thirties, but she could tell he was one of those men who would get better-looking as he got older. When she met his gaze again, she realized she wasn't bothered by his blatant stare because while it was calculating and yes, serious, she could tell that he was already leaning toward liking her, accepting her.

"What about you?" he asked.

"Pardon?"

"How did you come to art?"

She looked pointedly at the canvas. "I loved to paint, and wasn't half bad. But I don't have the magic. I've got an eye, though, and a reasonable talent for restoration. I found my place working on the business side."

He didn't respond, and she thought about glancing at him, but didn't. It would be easy to let herself get swept away by her physical reaction to him. The fact that she had responded to him at all was unsettling. She knew she was years away from being gobsmacked by looks, and she'd damn well better be past the stage where she got tongue-tied by wealth or power. She didn't even know if Noah had wealth or power. "You're a computer consultant?"

"White Hat Resources," he said. "My company specializes in neutralizing high-level computer threats."

"In other words, you're a hacker."

"Yes, exactly." He grinned. "We're the good guys."

"I imagine your services are in high demand."

He touched her arm again, in the very same spot. She did look up then. Excellent timing, as he led her to the next piece, by an artist Paige thought showed real promise.

"We're on the clock twenty-four/seven," he said. "It's a constant battle."

"And you're the boss, so all that pressure lands on your shoulders."

"Hence the need for art that moves me."

"I'd like to hear about your collection."

He turned to her, and she wasn't quick enough to glance away. Again, she was caught by him, drawn in. But just as he was about to speak, they were interrupted by a major donor to her museum. The man was the CEO of a huge corporation and had one of the great private art collections in the United States.

He shook Noah's hand, barely acknowledging her even though they'd had dealings. It was all right, though, as it gave her the opportunity to study Noah without being the deer caught in his headlights.

She wasn't the only one sizing up Noah. Mr. Saunders had skipped right over small talk and was asking about some foreign-sounding computer virus.

Noah frowned, took a half step closer to her, then very politely told Saunders that his company was aware of the threat, and that he'd be happy to set up a phone consult for Wednesday.

Saunders didn't care much for the brush-off, but made the appointment anyway. Noah graciously didn't gloat, in fact, he assured the man that his team would be in a better position to nullify the threat by Wednesday, so the timing was excellent.

It had been well-played, the whole encounter. She liked the way Noah handled himself. He was completely confident in his role and wore his power with elegance. Good to know.

"Sorry about that." He finished off his Scotch and looked at her wineglass. "Ready for another?"

She nodded, and they went in search of another bar. Unfortunately, they didn't get halfway there before they were approached by yet another titan of industry. He, too, wanted information and time with Noah, and the pattern continued over the next two hours.

Noah apologized, but there was little he could do short of being outright hostile. She'd have been a better sport if it had been easier to snack along the way, but carrying a tiny plate, a wineglass and her clutch while trying to look at art and be gracious when all she wanted to do was get Noah alone left her hungry and feeling cheated.

They'd almost finished the tour just as the auction came to a close. Noah stopped her before they left the annex, took her empty plate and almost empty glass and put them on a clearing tray. Then he took her hand in his and pulled her not toward the main showroom, but straight for the exit.

"This isn't working," he said, as he reached for the door. "I want to talk to you, and I can't here. Do you mind if we leave?"

She shook her head, glad to escape the interruptions, but a little nervous about their new destination.

He held the door for her and she went back out into the frigid night. They were at the rear of the gallery by the parking lot. He pulled a valet ticket out of his pocket. "The night hasn't gone quite the way I'd imagined. I don't know about you, but I'm hungry. And not for any more tiny food. How about we find something decent to eat? Somewhere quiet, where no one will know who we are."

As a shiver swept through her in the freezing night air, she grinned. "I'm in."

"Seafood? Steak? Italian?"

"Everything fancy's going to be booked to the gills. I vote for burgers."

"Good choice." He whipped off his tux jacket and put it around her shoulders, then pulled her close even as he walked them to the valet. "Then, after dinner, I'd like to take you back to my place."

# 3

As Noah gave the valet his tip, it occurred to him that his last statement left a lot of room for misinterpretation. As he walked around his car, he shook his head. He had this habit of leaping ahead in conversations, then neglecting to fill in the blank spots for the unfortunate person trying to follow along.

He slid on his seatbelt, then turned to Paige, wondering just how much trouble he was in. Her hand wasn't on the door, but her eyebrow was raised in subtle alarm, and her lovely lips had parted with the beginnings of a question. Such an expressive face.

He'd watched her closely in the gallery and her reactions to the art had been much more telling than her reactions to people. But that wasn't the point now, was it? "What I should have said was that if you're amenable, and it's not too late, I'd like you to come to see my collection, to get a feel for what I've got and what I'm hoping to do."

She continued to stare at him, but the eyebrow relaxed and she even managed a little grin. "Why don't we get some food. I'll be a lot more amenable after I have some fries."

"Great. Anywhere in particular you want to go?"

"Surprise me."

He released the Mercedes' brake, and merged into the smattering of traffic. "I'm something of a burger connoisseur, having lived off them for so many years. In between meals of mac and cheese and ramen noodles."

"Been there," she said. "College. And for a number of years after. They told me it built character, but I think that's a bunch of bull. All it did was give me lifelong cravings for food I swore I'd never eat again." She had relaxed into her seat, having apparently believed his explanation, and had even shifted her body so she could speak to him more easily. "French fries, though, they're my downfall."

He glanced at her, liking the way the city lights played over her face. "Am I contributing to the delinquency of an art specialist?"

"Yes. Completely. In fact, why don't you take all the guilt and let me eat in peace?"

"Done. I'll wring my hands at the first opportunity."

"Thanks. I appreciate it."

He turned on Van Ness, in no hurry despite his hunger. The evening so far had been…unexpected. It didn't exactly bother him that he'd found himself interested in this woman, but it did beg the question why. Paige was very attractive, there was no denying that. Maybe it was the combination of her blond hair and the vivid sky blue of her eyes. If he'd seen her across a room, he'd have never suspected that she was an art geek. It was shallow, he knew, but in his experience, women as beautiful as Paige preferred to look in mirrors, not at other people's art.

"Were you always a white hat?" she asked.

"I may have been a bit gray while I was finding my way," he said. "It's tempting, when you're a kid and you're good at code, to see what kind of mischief you can get away with."

"Were you ever caught?"

"Just the once was enough."

"Oh?"

"Nothing dramatic. I hacked into my brother's school and changed some of his records. He wanted to go to Harvard. I figured I could help."

"Did he get in trouble?"

"Nope. Just me. He did get into Harvard, without my assistance. I was without internet access for a year. Completely. It nearly drove me insane. Probably did, now that I think of it. I ended up designing code anyway. In my notebooks, by hand. I wasn't supposed to read magazines or books about computers, either, but I still managed to hear things. A year in the computer world is the equivalent of ten years in most other industries, and everything is life or death at sixteen, so I was terrified I'd never be able to catch up. I was better at computers than anything I'd ever done. I was scared spitless."

"And you've never crossed the line again?"

He smiled. "Not in any meaningful way. Certainly not with malicious intent."

"How come you weren't recruited by the FBI or CIA or something?"

"You watch too much television," he said.

"That was a non-answer."

He took advantage of the red light and looked at her full-on. "Yes, it was. I'm content with where I've ended up. For the most part. As with everything, there are compromises, challenges. Nothing's ever as perfect as we imagine it will be."

"That's true. Close is good, though."

"It is." He made the turn on Market, and in minutes they were parked in the lot for BurgerMeister.

"I thought this might be where we were headed," she said, the smile evident in her voice. "I love this place."

"I'm glad." He got out of the car and as he went around to open her door, he undid his tie and popped open the top two buttons of his shirt. Paige had let herself out, so he just locked up as she pulled his jacket tighter against the night. "You didn't bring a coat or...?"

"Funny story. I started out with a shawl. In fact, my favorite one. My only one. It met with an accident on the way to the gallery."

"Accident? You weren't—?"

"Only my feelings were hurt. It wasn't anyone's fault, unless you want to blame a particularly stubborn tree, the wind and the Municipal Transit System. I'll miss the shawl, but it wasn't a family heirloom or anything. You're probably freezing."

He put his arm around her shoulders again, more for her warmth than his, but he wasn't complaining. He liked holding her. The gallery had been full of the scents of flowers and perfumes, and now that he was close to her again, all he could smell was burgers. He wanted to know her scent, the feel of her skin, not his tux jacket. He also wanted to have her full attention when he told her something that mattered. It was crazy. Not like him, especially since the divorce. He'd have to be especially careful. Crazy had a way of getting him in real trouble.

They were able to get a table by the window. He sat across from her, as much to watch her as to keep a safe distance between them, although he supposed his precaution was futile considering he'd already invited her home.

To his surprise, neither of them needed menus, and Paige ordered his favorite meal, right down to the almost-burnt onions on the classic cheeseburger. She even asked for the strawberry shake. As far as deals went, this wasn't big, but it was a good sign.

The waiter left, and they were on their own again. There

wasn't much to see out the window, but the view from his seat was excellent. Not only could he look into her eyes, but her strapless dress showed off her lovely skin, including the enticing hint of her breasts above the blue material. He forced himself to look once again at her face, which was even more fascinating.

"I didn't ask," she said. "Did you put in any bids tonight?"

Noah nodded. "Two. Leon will call me tomorrow if I've won. They were both by an artist I'd only heard about. Daviel Shy. She's a filmmaker and illustrator as well as a painter. I'm impressed with what she does on canvas. I also donated a sculpture by Geoffrey Koetsch."

She narrowed her eyes. "You didn't mention that was your donation."

"I wanted your reaction without prejudice."

"How did I do?"

"Very well."

"As I recall," she said, "I didn't love it."

"No, you didn't. But you understood it. The reason I chose that particular piece for the fundraiser is because while I like it more than you, I have two other pieces by Koetsch that I prefer. I want to promote him, though. Not enough people know about what he's doing."

She leaned forward. He took another peek at her décolletage, but only a peek.

"Tell me," she said.

He did. It was a conversation, not a monologue, and while it was broken up by food arriving and food being eaten, it was the kind of discussion that was yet another layer of what kept him fascinated by art. Just as with computers and hacking, there was an insider language to art and collecting, one he was still learning after five years. Paige was tremendously knowledgeable, and just as impressively, she wasn't afraid to acknowledge what she didn't know.

Then the conversation started winding. From movies to plays to books. It surprised him that she was into science fiction, although he wasn't sure why. That got them talking about graphic novels and comics, and she'd actually read a number of them. Again, a surprise, which she pointed out was sexist. He'd have to think about that. He had some great female hackers in his shop, but none of them had ever talked about comics. Then again, he'd never brought the subject up.

When he finally looked around, they were the only two left in the restaurant. Paige seemed just as surprised. There was a small struggle over the bill, but he won, and then they were back in the car, the heater on full.

"I can't believe it's after eleven." He turned the key all the way, and listened to the purr of the engine, reluctant to say good-night.

"I know. The evening went by so fast."

"Too fast."

"Yes," she said softly, a streetlight illuminating her face and the uncertainty in her eyes. "And we haven't talked at all about your options with your collection," she added, tugging his lapels tighter around her shoulders.

"Cold?"

"What? No." She relaxed her grip.

"We can make an appointment for later in the week."

She frowned, and then gave her head a small shake. "Right," she said, but then she shook her head again, frowned. "Absolutely."

"Or, you could take a look at it now." He enjoyed the advantage of sitting in shadow while he watched her moisten her lush lips in frustration. She was probably trying to be sensible, and while he admired that, he was glad to see he wasn't the only one still thinking about his earlier invitation.

"We could…" she said, slowly enough that he knew now for certain she didn't want to put things off. And not just seeing his collection.

He let the silence alone. Totally ungentlemanly of him, but he needed this to be her decision. God knew he wasn't inclined to be sensible at the moment, because Paige made him want things he hadn't wanted in years. He was sure that if he stopped to analyze the feeling, he'd find it quite unsettling.

She glanced out the window, then stared down at her hands, her blossoming smile telling him that she was fully aware that while his invitation earlier had been mostly about art, that had been then. Now, it would be difficult for him to show her his home without wanting her to see his paintings in the morning light.

"We should make an appointment," she said finally.

"You're right, we should."

"I think we'd work well together. I know I'd enjoy it. If I come up to see your 'etchings,' things may get tricky."

Noah smiled. "It's a risk, all right."

Her mouth twisted wryly and she slumped deeper into his jacket.

"I do want to work with you," he added quickly. "But I won't lie. I'm extremely attracted to you."

She looked down, and while he couldn't see it, he would bet she was blushing. But then her head came up and her gaze met his. "You know what's got me worried?"

"What?"

"The fact that I'm here because of Curt."

"I don't understand."

"He did tell you we were together for a couple of years, didn't he?"

"He mentioned you'd broken up quite a while ago. Are you still—"

"Oh, no," she said, quickly, her expression making it clear she was telling him the truth. "We're better apart, trust me. What's getting to me is that he set this up. He's a pretty astute guy. He reads people well. I can't help wondering if this was his weird way of trying to get you to…"

"Sleep with his ex?"

"Hire him as your broker."

"Ah." He hadn't gotten that feeling the other night, but Paige knew Curt a lot better than he did. "If it turns out it was that second thing…deal breaker?"

She took a moment, and he used the opportunity to tell himself that he wouldn't press the issue. He wanted her to come home with him, wanted very much to see her without the beautiful dress, but the part of him that wasn't his dick knew that taking her home might be the best thing to do.

"No. Not a deal breaker." Paige touched his arm. "I've enjoyed tonight more than I ever expected to and for all kinds of reasons, only some of them having to do with business. On the other hand, my week has been the worst. I mean epically bad. Losing my shawl was the least of it."

Noah tried to hide a smile. "So you're expecting us to be that bad in bed?"

She laughed. "I see one has to be single-minded to be a hacker."

"Yes, I get your point." He turned his attention back to getting the car on the road, somewhat annoyed with himself. She was being a good sport, and he wasn't generally pushy. Not with women. "Where do you live?"

She hesitated, then gave him her address. "I've put you off," she said after they'd gone a mile.

He glanced at her in surprise. "I thought it was the other way around."

"Not at all." She shrugged. "I'm flattered. And very intrigued."

"So?" Damn, he was doing it again. "Okay, look, no pressure. We get to your place. I walk you to your door. You either kiss me on the cheek and then lock me out, or you run in and get a toothbrush."

Paige's soft laugh filled his chest with warmth. "Deal," she said and kept her gaze straight ahead, giving him not even the slightest clue as to what was going on in that pretty head.

# 4

THE WHOLE WAY TO HER APARTMENT, Paige told herself going to Noah's house would be a colossal mistake. It wasn't just the bad-luck run she'd been having, although that was probably enough of a reason to crawl into her own bed until Mercury was either in or out of retrograde, she could never remember which one made life suck. It was the mixing of business and pleasure.

She needed his business a lot more than she needed to sleep with him. He smiled at her as he made a right. The automatic squeezing of her legs and her accelerated heart rate begged to differ.

Only, this wasn't just about sex. Because this was not an ordinary man.

Before Curt, during another long dry spell, she and her friends had gotten together one rather drunken night and written out their perfect-man lists. There had been but one ground rule: they were to be as specific as hell. He must like dry wit but not bathroom humor; he can't be allergic to pets; art needs to play a significant role in his life; good, but not great at shooting pool. Like that. She couldn't re- member everything on her old list, but if she were to write one up now, Noah Hastings would have a whole lot of checkmarks to his credit.

If she did say no tonight, it wouldn't necessarily mean they wouldn't eventually get together. Pleasure should follow business, that was the wisest course. But the idea of postponing made her nervous. It wasn't logical, but then, intuition wasn't, was it? If it was intuition and not hormones in overdrive.

No. Intuition. This was a defining moment.

There were no guarantees. He might end up being someone totally wrong for her, or he could screw her both literally and figuratively and never speak to her again. The possibilities for a bad outcome far outweighed the chances for magic. Still…

"This is your street?"

She snapped out of her trance and saw it was, in fact, her street. There was her car, the one she'd decided not to take because she was certain not to find a better parking space. "You know what?" she said, as the car slowed way down.

"What?"

"I would like to go see your collection."

Was that a sigh of relief? Or wishful thinking? It definitely was a smile.

"Terrific," he said, and hit the accelerator.

"Wait." Laughter bubbled up past her lips. While it was tempting to tease him about his enthusiasm, she said, "Since we're here I'd like to run in and get some things."

"Right. Of course." He backed up the car.

"There's a spot on the right, see it?" She pointed.

He slid into the space that was directly in front of her front steps. "You want company?"

"Thank you, no. I'll just be a minute."

"I'll be waiting."

She moved to open her door, but stopped at the hand on her arm. She turned back, and then his lips were touching hers, softly, asking permission. Whether she gave it to him by a breath or her shiver, she didn't know or care because he deepened the kiss, letting her feel his intention. Her lips parted and he sneaked inside, tasting good and warm.

The last of her doubts fled as his hand slipped behind her neck, his fingers cool and sure. Although he kept the pressure light and his tongue hesitant, there was a banked tension in the shoulder she gripped that matched the way her chest had tightened. She wanted more, but not here, and not quite yet. The climax of the evening might be known, but the dance was still to come, and she didn't want to give up a single second of that.

When he pulled back, her eyes stayed closed until she caught her breath. When she did look, it was to see his gentle smile, his eyes alight from more than just the street-lamp. "I'll be waiting," he repeated, his voice lower and holding far more promise.

This time, she made it out the door, giddy with what she was about to do. Not the getting-her-stuff-together part, but spending the rest of the night with Noah. That was plenty to be giddy about.

She was up the building's steps in a dash, then in the elevator, her fingers tapping on her dress as she ascended, wanting the door to open, wanting to be done with tooth-brushes and makeup. Three words circled over and over in her head: "This is crazy." But it wasn't a warning. It was wicked, like smoking in the girls' bathroom or spiking the prom punch. She'd been in charge of the decorations at her own prom, and wicked was hardly part of her repertoire, which she imagined was a large part of the thrill. As long as she was going to disregard a lifelong pattern, she couldn't think of a more delicious man to do it with.

Everything that was going in her overnight bag was in it, including an outfit for work tomorrow, and if she forgot something major, so be it. She thought about changing clothes, but only for a second. She did grab her coat so she could return Noah's jacket. Only because she had to, though.

She couldn't get over this *feeling*. Breathless, foolish, nuts, tingly, hyper. Everything she made a point not to be. This whole business was risky and stupid, and it was like a tonic, a cure for everything that ailed her. She wasn't quite so far gone as to think it was anything like love at first sight or destiny, but she didn't really need it to be.

She was about to break a whole boatload of rules. Damn the consequences. For her, that was saying a whole lot. She was all about the consequences, but even when she planned things out to the last detail—figured out every angle, made smart moves, did her homework—it could all end up in the toilet. Kandinsky anyone?

Her own giggle surprised her. She grabbed her purse, her bag and her jacket, and she was out of there. Her fingers shook as she locked her door. The elevator slowed on purpose, but then she was flying down the steps and he was still there in his sleek black Mercedes and the passenger door swung open before she hit the sidewalk.

Holy crap.

TALK ABOUT UNEXPECTED. As he watched her swing her bag into his back seat, Noah thought that of all the possible outcomes of tonight's fundraiser, Paige coming home with him was the least likely. But damn, he was pleased. She was ridiculously pretty. Better still, she was someone he could talk to. Not about computers, no, but then he had a lot of people in his life who wanted to talk about those. She knew art. She knew good cheeseburgers. She'd read

*Watchman* and *Locke and Key*. Better even than that, when he looked her in the eyes, there was a spark.

Maybe it was all about sex, and in the morning he'd be able to think more clearly. That would be a decision for tomorrow. Tonight, the moment he'd pulled out onto the street, he reached for her hand.

"Where are you taking me?"

"Pacific Heights."

"Really?"

He heard the layers of her comment. "Yes, I'm a decadent capitalist. No excuses."

"I'm not asking for any. I'd already gathered that thwarting hackers was lucrative."

"It is."

"Just so you know, I'm going to hit you up for a lot more donations than I'd intended. I hope you have a huge collection."

"Not yet. But some day I'd like to."

"Good. I'm quite ruthless. Not just for the museum, either. I'm tough when it comes to protecting art. Seriously protective."

"Yet another reason I want to work with you. I don't want to lose another painting."

"A theft?"

"A divorce. She didn't even like the work particularly. But she knew I did."

"Ouch. How long ago?"

"Just this year, although we hadn't lived together for the last three. She's in L.A. doing something in the recording industry, I'm not clear on it."

"I'm sorry."

"Don't be. It's better this way. I only thought we had a lot in common. I was young."

"I thought hackers didn't even date, let alone get married young," she said.

"I'm a rebel."

She squeezed his hand. "I'm still sorry. I know what it's like to have a broken heart." She paused. "On the other hand, I also know how good it can feel to leave when it's not working out."

"Curt."

"Precisely."

"I never knew him well, but we had some good times."

"That's pretty much how I felt just before I broke it off."

That made him glance at her, and sure enough, a wry smile and one lifted eyebrow let him know she wasn't kidding. He liked this woman.

His gaze went back to the road.

She leaned toward him. "I want to know more about you."

"Ask away," he said, only wincing on the inside at his recklessness.

"Okay. Tell me one of your favorite memories from childhood."

Unexpected. Again. He had to think about it. He'd had a good childhood. Not perfect, but none ever were. His parents, though, had been young and adventurous. They hadn't really been surprised that he'd been caught hacking. Or that he'd turned it into his profession. Ah. "My folks used to take spontaneous road trips. They'd wake me and my brother in the middle of the night from time to time, and we'd all climb in my father's ancient VW van. Someone would pick a direction, and off we'd go.

"West was out, as we lived near the beach, but that still left a lot of territory. They had no problem with us missing a few days of school, either. They considered the trips educational, and sometimes they even were. Once, we were gone for two weeks. We'd only packed for the night, so that was interesting. I was lucky. My parents are remarkable people, and they taught me a lot about independence and self-reliance."

"Wow. That's impressive. I like your folks."

He smiled. "So do I. They live in France now. I try to get out to see them at least once a year."

They'd made good time and were getting close to his place, but he liked this part, and didn't want it to end too quickly. "Your turn."

"Baking with my mom," she answered, quickly. As if she'd known her answer before she'd asked the question. "It was just us for most of my life. My father died when I was seven, and Mom worked a lot, but she found time for us. We would spend hours in the kitchen, making everything from bread to cakes to my personal favorite, cookies. Man, her chocolate chip cookies are still the best I've ever tasted. But that's probably because they're so full of good memories."

"Does she live near you?"

"Santa Clara. She works for the department of water and power."

"So you're close?"

"Yep."

Wrapped in comfortable silence, they climbed the hills in his neighborhood until they were almost at the summit. He slowed as he pressed the garage door open, and then pulled into the space, parking between his bike and the Jeep.

"I can't believe you have a garage. That is awesome."

"Spoken like a true San Franciscan." He turned off the engine and went around to open her door. She let him this time, even let him grab her bag. He liked it that even though she'd brought a jacket, she hadn't taken his off.

Then again, he wished she had when he touched the small of her back as they entered the house. Important information could be gleaned from that simple maneuver, and his data wasn't complete through the material. Had her skin shimmied? Would he have felt her heat? He needed to try it again, later.

Without a touch or the flip of a switch, the downstairs lights went on. Because he was and would always be a computer geek, he'd wired the place himself, making the most of automation. There were sensors throughout that would turn on lights, open or close blinds, lock and unlock doors and windows, pipe in music. A side benefit was the wow factor, which Paige demonstrated with wide eyes and parted lips.

They walked through the kitchen, her steps slowing as they passed the fancy stuff the designer added not for him, as he wasn't a particularly avid cook, but for his ex-wife. At the thought, he parted from Paige, putting her bag on the dining-room table while she was still checking out the deep-pot sink.

"You like wine?"

She nodded.

"Great. Why don't we find a bottle together. The cellar is next to the art room."

She stared at him more intently than she had at the sink.

"You have an art room."

"Temperature- and humidity-controlled."

"And a wine cellar."

He shrugged. "What can I say? Malicious hackers keep on coming."

"Show me."

He took her through the living room, where he removed his jacket from her shoulders, to the stairs, self-conscious now about the elevator. That had been installed for Mary's parents, who'd never ended up staying with them. Paige paused, staring back at the view. One whole wall was glass, and the city glittered below them. "We'll come back up," he said.

"Bet your ass we will," she said, her lack of reserve making him grin.

After a short wind down the circular staircase, he pressed his thumb on the biometric lock before he opened the cellar door. This room was all his. The redwood racks held over two hundred bottles, and the arches were all hand carved. Even the tasting table had been done to his specifications. "What's your pleasure?"

"Ogling."

"And to drink while you ogle?"

"I'm going to let you choose."

"Merlot?"

"Perfect."

She wandered as he picked out a particularly fine vintage. Before she'd made a complete tour, he'd poured them each a glass. She took hers, and he watched her face as she went through all the steps—the swirling, the sniff, added rolling her eyes in an expression of bliss—before she sipped. "Oh, man. This is amazing."

"I'm glad you like it," he said, stepping closer to her. He let her have one more sip before he took her glass and put it down next to his. Her surprise quelled as he pulled her into his arms. Now he could feel her body's reaction to his touch. The shimmy was there, all right, even before his lips came down on hers.

# 5

SHE TASTED THE WINE on his tongue, and decided that given the choice, she'd always order by the kiss instead of the glass. She clutched at his shoulder, not just in reaction to the way his mouth moved on hers, but because of the fact that she was here, that an hour ago they'd been eating burgers, that she was kissing this remarkable man at all.

It felt as if this were someone else's life. Hers was filled with lost shawls and long days and a lonely apartment. This was so unlikely, it made her think not of the man who was kissing her, but of the man who'd put them together.

He pulled away, not far. "Are you okay?"

She straightened, startled by his question. "Yes. Why?"

"I had you," he said, as his finger gently swept her cheek. "I had you, and then…"

"I guess I'm a little overwhelmed."

He stepped back and her hand dropped from his crisp white shirt. "I'm sorry."

"Why?"

He picked up her glass and handed it to her, then got his own. "I guess this wasn't such a great idea. We just met and—"

"I wanted to come."

He winced. "I got caught up in—" He looked up as if searching the ceiling for what he was trying to say. When he finally met her gaze again, it was only for a second. "This was inappropriate. I apologize. I should take you home."

He turned, his glass hitting the table too hard.

She didn't even think, she just grabbed his arm. "Wait. Stop. I'm here because I want to be."

First he stared at her hand, then at her. "We'll be working together, at least I hope we will. I can't promise that because I don't know everything I need to about the museum or what your proposal will be. But if it happens or it doesn't, it's not dependent on you being here. Staying here tonight."

"I figured that out before I said yes."

"I certainly never meant to overwhelm you."

She smiled, even though she knew the magic bubble had popped. "The overwhelm has nothing to do with your art collection. Trust me."

He looked around. "We should have stayed at your place. Mine is a bit much."

"It's fabulous. And the only wine I have is a perky little number from New Zealand that's not in the same universe as what you've got here. But it's not about the house, which is beautiful, by the way."

"Then what?"

Paige thought about what she should tell him, but after a few seconds she realized the only thing she could tell him was the truth. "The whole night. I didn't expect you."

"No?"

She shook her head. "It's difficult because it was Curt's idea. I don't know what your past with him was like, but with me, he had a real talent for manipulating me to get what he wanted. He was damn good at it, too. It took me a long time to catch on. But I did, in the end. Nothing is straightforward with him, and while he claimed he was just trying to apologize for some things he said, I can't be sure. He knows art, so I wasn't dismissing the idea that your collection would be great, but I never dreamed I would feel so...drawn to you."

He exhaled a big breath. "Now that I think about it, he did get a lot of help with his schoolwork. As I recall, some people claimed he didn't even take his own finals."

"All done cheerfully by women, I'm guessing."

Noah shrugged. "I don't know what his motives were in setting the two of us up. All I can tell you is that there is no hidden agenda on my part. I have several million dollars sunk into my collections, and I want to protect them and my investments. As far as being attracted to each other, I don't believe that's something Curt could manipulate."

"I don't know. He's pretty good."

"Not this good. I watched you walk into the gallery, and all I could think of was how much I wanted you to be Paige Callahan."

Her breath hitched. "Really?"

He nodded and his body relaxed.

"I was awfully glad you turned out to be you, too. And not just because you're pretty, either."

He chuffed out a laugh. "Pretty?"

"Fine. Handsome. If it had only been that, though, I wouldn't have come."

"So you really came for my etchings?"

"I'm trying to be serious and honest here."

"Sorry."

"I'm twenty-seven, Noah. I've been around the block a couple of times. I appreciate beauty, but it isn't nearly enough to entice me to bed."

"So, I'm more than just beefcake, huh?"

"The beefcake doesn't hurt, but yes. I haven't done anything like this in…well, ever."

"Never? What about college?"

"I was a stick-in-the-mud. Always studying. A wild night for me was going to the coffeehouse with my friends. I got too little sleep, worried too much, but I graduated summa cum laude. And…that tells you pretty much everything about me in a nutshell. Not terribly glamorous."

"No keggers?"

"Not a one."

"No boys?"

"A couple. Nothing noteworthy. Nice guys, though. I was more interested in school than anything else. My mother said I was a late bloomer. But then, she's my mom."

Noah touched her arm, but didn't move closer. "I believe you've blossomed into someone quite remarkable."

Her whole body flushed with a warm heat that started at her core. She cleared her throat, not wanting to derail the conversation, not when there was more to say. She wanted him to know who she was, and why staying wasn't a light decision for her. "The point is even when I was supposed to be reckless, I wasn't. I'm careful. With my safety and with my feelings. The only thing I'm impulsive about is shoes. Ask any of my friends. They're constantly trying to get me to shake loose. Get wild. I disappoint them so often, I'm surprised we're all still friends. I mean, I even hate my own surprise parties. So tonight is kind of off-script."

"I see."

She looked down, but he lifted her chin with the side of his hand. "No, I really see. You've just described me, fairly accurately."

"What?"

"It makes more sense now, this attraction. Except for the

shoe fetish and my friends trying to loosen me up, you and I are eerily alike. I back-up my work every twenty seconds. I don't like surprises. And I don't make a habit of bringing home beautiful women I've just met."

"Really?" she asked, but it wasn't a question. More a doubt.

"That surprises you?"

"With a bachelor pad like this? Yeah, it kinda does."

"I didn't build it as a babe magnet." He ran his hand over the tasting table. "This was supposed to be the last house I'd ever own. Where my children would grow up. Where I'd celebrate my fiftieth wedding anniversary. Didn't quite work out that way."

"You built it for her."

He took a sip of wine before he spoke. "I rushed things with Mary. We didn't sleep together on the first night, in fact, not for the first few weeks. But I didn't get to really know her. She didn't care for my hours. What had seemed exotic and a little dangerous in the beginning wasn't so pleasant when the blush was off the rose. She did like the money. I thought the house would bring us closer. For a while it did. She loved working with the architect and the designers. But when it came down to just the two of us in this big old house, there wasn't a lot to say."

"I really am sorry. At least you got a fantastic house out of it. I mean it, this is spectacular, and I've only seen a few rooms. I can't imagine what the upstairs is like."

He turned, got a bottle stopper out of a drawer and recorked the wine. "Still want to see my etchings?"

"Very much."

"Okay." He didn't move though, not for a long moment. "Let's just see where the night takes us, all right? Maybe it'll lead to the bedroom—and a large part of me hopes like hell it will—but I'd like it to be fine with both of us if it doesn't."

The butterflies in her stomach took her by surprise. She almost laughed when she realized she was having a major sexual response to a man telling her he wanted to be cautious. "I'm good with that."

"Also?" he said, still not moving along.

"Hmm?"

"You're stunning."

She felt the compliment all the way to her toes and had to bite back a huge happy sigh. Not because the words were so nice, but because the way he'd said them brought the magic bubble back. In spades.

NOAH WALKED HER ACROSS the basement to the art-preservation room, still a little shaken from their conversation. He understood Paige's concern about Curt setting this up, understood her all too well. It had got him thinking about just what the hell *he* was doing. He hadn't just invited her into his home, he was about to bare part of his soul.

He'd had almost the whole property redecorated after Mary left. Although he'd built it for a dying marriage, it had become his pride and joy. It startled him to realize how much he wanted Paige to approve.

He had iris-recognition on this room, which to his mind was superior to the biometric fingerprint systems. Once the camera scanned his eye, the door opened, and with some trepidation, he held it for Paige.

He wanted her to like his paintings, maybe more than he wanted her to like the house. Normally, he didn't give a shit. His taste was his own. But just as he'd been pleased when she'd ordered "his" cheeseburger, he wanted that same rush again. He wanted to see pleasure on her face.

"This is like a small museum," she said, entering the

space with careful steps, looking around at the walls, all painted the same matte white, the better to show off the intricacies and the colors of the paintings.

He walked with her, reading her as she slowed and studied each of his twenty-six canvases. They didn't speak, and that was good. Talking was for later.

This was how he viewed fine art. Quietly, in his own world. He loved the way his brain reacted to different paintings, skittering from sensation to memory to emotion.

But as she moved from the dark de Kooning to the vibrancy of John Ferren, she changed along with the tones of the work. He could see it not just in the set of her mouth, but her posture, the way her fingers held her wineglass. The cant of her head was extraordinarily telling.

If she didn't love the work itself, he already knew she understood it to her bones.

Dammit, he wanted her more than ever. That should be warning enough. He was behaving like a lunatic tonight. Running out on the fundraiser, sweeping this stranger away to a burger joint, bringing her here. Not his house—here. To this room. It was as intimate to him as his bedroom, sometimes more so. This was his passion unveiled. His heart. Some of his longest acquaintances hadn't ever seen the inside of this room.

In front of every canvas were two chairs. Incredibly comfortable chairs, placed at the optimal distance. She stood next to the chairs at each stop, then moved in front of them. He heard her sigh, more than once. Long, satisfied exhalations.

She *saw*.

When they were at the door again, she turned to him, studied him as she had his art. She touched the edge of his mouth with the soft pad of her thumb. "The collection is magnificent. I love your eyes."

This time, when he kissed her, she melted into him, and he into her.

# 6

THE WAY HE CUPPED the back of her head was almost as good as the way he kissed her.

He nibbled on her bottom lip, teasing her with his tongue until she whimpered. No, the kiss was better. His hand at her neck was wonderful, careful and urgent all at once, but his kiss made her stomach swoop and her knees grow weak.

But her stolen breath and wobbly knees weren't only from the slow slide of their tongues. She was knocked out by the house, the beauty of his art, the San Francisco night, the taste of merlot. The way she wanted him so much she ached.

Paige ran her hand down his long back, over his shoulder blade. His muscles bunched as he moved against her. He was hard all over. She was sure she couldn't really feel the heat of him through their clothes, but this wasn't reality. Not hers, anyway.

Noah pulled back. "Upstairs?"

She nodded, but he was already on his way to the wine room to gather the bottle and their glasses. Once back at her side, he offered her his arm. Together, they walked up the stairs. On the main floor, she retrieved her overnight bag. Her attention was pulled by the spectacular view, but only for a moment.

More stairs, beautiful artwork in the hallway, especially the Gorky. And then his bedroom.

She'd expected special but she got spectacular. Huge. Two walls were entirely glass, and the view of the city lights was captivating. She was vaguely aware that he slipped her bag from her hand, but she was already walking toward the free-standing fireplace that was nestled in a sculpture that would have been at home in her museum. The black-and-rust bedroom felt masculine, but not overly so. His bed rested on a platform that drew her gaze straight to the large canvas above it. It was an abstract, dark but dreamy, hypnotizing. The whole room was. Everywhere she looked, there was something wonderful, something astonishing. Especially when she looked up at Noah.

"Thank you," he whispered. "For being here."

"It's…" She didn't have the right words. So she kissed him instead.

His hands went to her shoulders, then skimmed down her arms in a feathery touch. When she shivered, he moaned. His fingers met at her back, at the top of her zipper. "Yes?"

She nodded quickly, anxious to get back to his lips. This kiss was short, as quick as it took him to undo her dress. She pressed her arms to her sides to keep the gown from falling. "The windows."

"No one can see in," he said. "No one can see you but me." He took hold of her hand and led her toward the junction of the two windows. Her entire field of vision was a panorama of the hills of San Francisco alive with light and motion.

Noah stepped back, slightly behind her. When she shifted her focus she could see him clearly in the window, herself as well. It was as if she were standing on the precipice of two worlds, the vast breadth of the stunning city at her feet and the breathless intimacy of the man about to touch her.

His hand rested warmly on her bare shoulder. His gaze met hers in the glass. She let go of everything but this moment. Relaxed her arms and watched as her dress slipped down her body, leaving her almost naked as if she were a piece of art herself, with swirls of blue puddled at her feet.

She heard his breath stutter, watched him look at her reflection. He brought his free hand to her other shoulder as he stepped just a bit closer. Close enough for her to feel his warmth.

The surreality was made even more intense by the fact that Noah was still dressed. She wanted him naked, yes, but something about this tableau felt more erotic just as it was. Naked would come, but right now she wanted to be here.

His hands brushed slowly down her arms. Not delicate enough to tickle, not hard enough to feel the texture of his skin. He moved slowly again, up the front of her arms to her neck then lower to her chest, watching carefully, as if he were sculpting her. His gaze didn't meet hers, and she wondered if he had been looking straight at her if she'd have seen the way he hungered.

He made her feel beautiful, extraordinary. She stood perfectly still as he continued to skim over her body, every angle, every curve. The only time he touched her was when he reached her hips. Carefully, as if unwrapping a rare gift, he lowered her panties, letting them fall to the tangle of her dress.

She refocused on her body. When was the last time she'd really seen herself? Months? Years? And never like this. As though she were looking through his eyes. The flaws had been the only things for so long. This was a revelation. She didn't look airbrushed or like the models in the magazines. She was fuller, less symmetrical. When he floated his palms over the soft roundness of her tummy, she didn't suck it in, paused but for a second to banish her inner critic.

He only went as low as his arms would reach. More, she thought, because his view would have been blocked than because he didn't want to.

Instead, he repeated the journey in reverse, only this time, he touched her. She gasped when she felt his hands on her upper thighs. He was warm, and big. Masculine hands so dark against her pale flesh. She couldn't see all of him, so she focused on his face. The term *lantern-jawed* could be used to describe him, but that wasn't enough. It didn't come close to describing how everything about his face worked. Of course, she would notice things like his symmetry and proportions. She'd been trained to look. But it was more than a surface beauty. There was intelligence in his eyes. He listened with his whole self. There hadn't been a moment when she'd thought he was simply waiting for his turn to talk. That shouldn't have made him better-looking, but it did.

She trusted him. It was too soon for that. She shouldn't. Hadn't Curt taught her anything? But there it was. She stood still as a statue and let him strip her after knowing him for mere hours, and she felt completely safe. Without doubt, if she said to stop right now, she knew he would. That he would take her home, and make an appointment to meet at the museum.

That made him gorgeous.

He drew her gaze back to the window when he lingered where her thighs met her torso. On each side, he drew a slow line, back and up, down to the edges of her pubic hair. Again. Defining that space, that line. And when she looked at his face, his lips had parted as he stared, his breath on her shoulder hot and needful. But it was his gaze that made her gasp. The want made her head swim, her body moist.

Dizzy at the sensory overload, she refocused on the distance. On the lights of the city. As she stared at the night it felt colder everywhere but where his hands held her.

He stepped closer, touching her, warming her now with his body against her back. The softness of his shirt belied the hardness of his chest. The cool shirt buttons were a tiny shock. The way his erection pushed at his pants was no shock at all.

"I want you," he whispered, his lips nearly brushing the shell of her ear.

"Yes," she said through a sigh, but she didn't turn. Not yet. She closed her eyes, wanting only to feel him for a moment. To sink below the water of darkness into pure sensation.

She wondered what her goosebumps felt like to his fingertips, to his palms.

But he clearly didn't want to wait, not for her to swim up again to light, because he turned her, pulled her into his arms. She opened her eyes just as he bent to kiss her.

# 7

NOAH CLOSED HIS EYES as he thrust his tongue inside her willing mouth. He was mad to get her in bed, to get rid of his clothes, to have her, and no one to blame but himself.

She was nothing less than exquisite, and seeing her mirrored in the glass had given him an experience he'd remember for the rest of his life. Odd that he'd never brought a woman here, to this spot, not even his ex-wife, when it was so obvious a thing to do.

Now, though, he didn't want to think of anyone else, not even in passing, not when the wealth of Paige was his for the taking.

He pulled back from her, met her clear, blue eyes. "I thought I was overwhelmed before," she said. "Now..."

"Do you want me to stop?" He knew even as he said the words that it might kill him if she said yes.

"No. I want to see you. All of you."

He smiled, more than happy to oblige. Perhaps it would have been more dramatic and more fitting for him to slowly disrobe, but he'd run out of patience the moment she'd pressed against him.

His cuffs gave him trouble, but it only lasted long enough for him to walk her to the edge of the bed. Then his shirt was on the floor, his pants undone with a bit more care, seeing as he was achingly hard. He pulled off everything else in a blur, but finally, he was as naked as she was.

Paige sat, her back straight, a small smile curving her lips as she took her sweet time giving him a once-over. He had to give her this. For God's sake, he'd just spent who knows how long studying her as if she were the Venus de Milo.

It wasn't comfortable, but he didn't really mind. He kept himself in shape, although he wouldn't be on the cover of *Fitness* any time soon. Though if it had been anyone else, he would have made an excuse, gotten on the bed, done something other than just stand there, not daring to look down. He knew his cock was sticking out like a flag pole, and that if her gaze dipped any lower, the flag might just wave. Her eyes kept him steady.

She looked at him the same way she'd looked at his art. As he'd looked at her. Not as a trinket but something worthwhile that deserved study. That brought heat to his face, and while he owed her a lot more time, he couldn't take it another minute. Just as she reached crotch level, he caved, and joined her on the bed. He'd meant to pull down the spread, but he needed to touch her now, arrange things later.

She laughed as she fell back, her hair spreading over the dark duvet in a halo of soft gold.

"Okay, fine. But come on. You're so much more interesting and beautiful to look at."

Her fingers brushed his cheek, then carded through his hair. "I beg to differ."

He looked down at her. "There's no contest."

"We'll have to agree to disagree. And thank you. But it wasn't just you enjoying the view. Standing there was an out-of-body experience. It didn't even feel like me reflected in the glass. I saw in a whole new way. That's not something that happens every day. So thank you for that, too."

He kissed her gently. "I don't think I'll ever stand in that corner again without seeing you in the window."

Her lips parted and her eyes widened for a second. The next second she moved, her fingers touching his jaw. "I want more," she said, as her nail moved slowly down his neck to his chest, where she flattened her palm near his heart.

The next kiss wasn't gentle. It was open-mouthed and needy, met with her own urgency. His hand went to her breast, cupping her, feeling the contrast between her hard nipple and the softness around it. Everything about her felt soft to him. Soft and curved, with none of his sharp angles or jutting bones. Even as he kissed her luscious mouth he wanted to move, to taste everything.

He gave in, sliding his lips down her delicate jaw and spending too little time on her neck, promising himself that he would return there later. But now he licked the flat of his tongue over her nipple before he took the edges of her aureole between his teeth and he swirled and sucked, moaning as his senses were filled with her taste, and finally, her scent.

Paige arched her back, shivering and gasping at his intensity. She was being ravished, and whatever her experiences in her past had been, this was something new. He was patient, clever, wicked. Very, very thorough. It was only after her heart stopped threatening to beat out of her chest that she was able to continue her own explorations. Her hand moved down his warm chest, up his side, down his cool back. Everywhere there was muscle just beneath the surface, tensing, releasing. The breadth of his chest was felt half by her body, half by her palm.

Even this, what should be just having sex, wasn't in

any way what she expected. It was layers of learning him, depths of perception as if she'd been given new and startling senses. She felt him tremble as if it was the only thing that was happening. At the same time her body was swept away by his lips and tongue and heat as if the entire world was him sucking her nipple.

Odd and perfect, she could hardly imagine what it would be like to have him inside her. At that thought, she had no choice. Her hand went from the top of his ass straight to his cock.

It was his turn to gasp, to arch, and she liked that she'd surprised him. He wasn't the only one who could shake things up.

"God, what are you doing?"

"I would think it was kind of obvious."

He looked at her, his eyes ablaze with a kind of delighted shock. "You... I was..."

She scooted down the bed until they were eye to eye. "I want all of it. I swear, I do. But I want you inside me."

He didn't blink, but his lips curved into a smile that was more than a little sinful. "I can do that."

"If it's no trouble."

His chuckle was a roll of soft wonder from her chest on down. Her hiss, when his grip abandoned her breast to thrust two fingers into her wet heat, made him laugh again.

"Touché," she said, although her voice sounded unnaturally breathy.

He kissed her as he shuffled them until he was looking down at her, his knees easing her legs farther apart. He'd gone for the missionary position. It seemed so normal after a night of surprises. But she was glad of it because she wanted to see him, watch his face as they made love.

And there was another revelation. Not many hours ago,

they hadn't met. They were complete strangers. She'd had no idea what Noah looked like. She'd felt too close to desperate about a potential acquisition and highly suspicious of Curt's involvement. That it was Valentine's Day had made everything worse. She'd been so sure it would all end in disaster. "Who'd have thought," she whispered.

He had braced himself on one elbow, his free hand meandering down her belly. "That this would happen?"

She nodded.

His smile was wry. "You were my safety date. Valentine's is a dangerous day for a man who wants no involvement. It's almost as bad as taking a date to a wedding."

His fingers brushed over her lower lips, a ghost touch that made her eyes close as she shivered. His smile had gone by the time she looked at him again. His gaze had darkened so much. He wanted her, it was all over the tense lines of his face, the way his chest rose and fell, how he dripped his hot excitement onto her inner thigh.

He pulled away, back. She gripped his arm, whimpered with the loss.

"One second. Two at the most."

He leaned over and reached for the side of the bed, and she realized. Condom. Important. But dammit.

"See. I'm already back." He ripped open the packet with his teeth.

"Would you like a hand?"

"No. Thank you."

He pushed himself up onto his knees so she had to lift her head to watch him as he rolled the rubber down. He winced as he did so; his penis jerked. He took advantage of his position to let his gaze roam. She couldn't blame him, as she did exactly that, but her impatience peaked with an inner pulse.

"Noah."

"Just torturing myself," he said. "I'm like a geek in an Apple store."

She grinned. "Wow. I've never been compared to electronics before."

He was over her, kissing her. "It's a compliment."

"I believe you."

"I want you," he said, his voice lower. Rougher.

"I believe that, too."

He thrust inside her, not stopping until he filled her. Even with him studying her, she didn't hide a thing. Not her moan, not the biting of her lower lip, not even her fingers digging hard into his back.

His slide soon quickened as he pushed and withdrew. Each time he came into her, he went all the way and each time, she lifted to meet him. It still wasn't enough. She wrapped her legs around his slim hips, let herself feel his muscles beneath her calves.

Part of her wanted to close her eyes. It flashed through her mind that she'd always closed her eyes, always focused on the sensations coursing through her body. Tonight she needed the connection more.

As she had at the window, she became a little dizzy with this heightened awareness. She'd naturally fallen into the rhythm of his breathing, so when his chest expanded, hers contracted. The smell of him, spicy and masculine, mixed with the scents of sex to make a new perfume that swirled in the heated air.

She loosened her grip on him but only so she could touch new places. She stole a bead of sweat from his temple. Tasted him, the salt sharp and intimate on her tongue. She touched his lips and he captured her finger between his teeth, rolling his tongue, sucking her.

With her free hand, she reached low, to the side of his

bottom just so she could feel the dimple when he thrust. He moaned low and long as she squeezed his cock.

Still their gazes held. He stared into her, releasing her finger as his hips moved faster, harder. Then, despite her resolve, the muscles in her body tightened, pulling her up and up, stealing her very breath...

Her eyes closed as she cried out.

# 8

HE GASPED WHEN SHE CAME. His body trembled in the war between watching her and finishing himself. He was close, so close. But she was incredible. Her pale skin flushed, her eyes danced beneath her lids, her mouth opened in a cry that tore at his chest.

Noah looked down, caught by the lines in her neck, but more focused now on the way his balls were tightening.

It was no good, he had to close his eyes. He'd think later.

His hips moved faster, he thrust deeper, harder, and there it was, the point of no return, the moment he wanted to freeze in time, to feel *this* forever. Everything tensed and his cry came from somewhere deep as he threw back his head, straining, stilling as the orgasm slammed. Starbursts flared as the tremors went on and on until he was empty, exhausted.

He wanted to let go, crash down, but she was under him, and she was smiling at him. One kiss, quick, because he needed air, to be continued when he stopped panting.

A hiss as he withdrew, not from discomfort but because he hated leaving that wet heat. Then he was on his back, next to her. Sweat cooled him down quickly, but didn't stop his gulping air. She was gasping, too. They were both grinning like fools.

"I should go clean up," he said, not surprised that he sounded drunk.

She nodded. "Probably."

"Can't move just yet."

"Uh-huh."

He barked out a laugh at how wrecked they both were. For a couple of minutes, they both just breathed. But he found her hand and she threaded her fingers between his.

"That was... Wow."

"Uh-huh."

"I mean," she said, turning to look at him, "unbelievable. So much happened."

His grin grew. He knew exactly what she meant. "It was a goddamned banquet."

She nodded, a bit of her hair falling from one edge of the pillow to another.

"I really need to get up. Before I fall asleep."

"Sucks to be you."

He laughed again, and that did it. He let her go and forced himself upright.

In the bathroom, he took care of business as his mind settled back into a more regular rhythm. He thought about taking a quick shower, but he was too tired, and he wanted to be back in bed. Next to Paige. Get them under covers, make sure she was comfortable. Sleep with her beside him.

Shit. He didn't like sharing his bed, not for sleep. He was doing it again. Wanting too much, too quickly. It had been the most intense sexual experience of his life, including his first time with his ex-wife. But this was when he needed to be careful. For all his logic, he could be a sentimental idiot. He'd let his dick do the thinking when he'd fallen for

Mary, and he couldn't do that again. Despite the fact that he wanted more, much more, of Paige.

He needed to pull back. Just take a step away, as hard as that would be. Not too far, though, because what if...?

They had the art to work on. Meetings. Lawyers. That would help, that would be great. They could still have lunch together. Dinners. Sex. He would take it slowly. Not jump into anything they'd both regret.

But he didn't have to step back tonight. She was still in his bed. Warm. Beautiful. Soft and sweet and God, the way she smelled and made him laugh.

With his hands full of soap, it dawned on him. He wanted to be careful with Paige. Not for his sake, but for hers. For *theirs*. There was a chance here for something important. He wasn't willing to screw it up.

He grabbed a towel and dried himself off, his smile back in place. He wanted her. More than he'd wanted anything in years.

PAIGE CURLED AROUND Noah's long, lean body, her head pillowed by his chest. She was wrung out and exhausted, but incredibly happy. She wanted the night to last forever. But sleep stole her away before the next breath.

When she woke, it was to light. To warmth. To Noah's body pressed against her back, his arm around her waist. The last of her dream skittered away, and she wasn't sorry, even though it had been a great dream. This was better.

He stirred next to her, grumbled something she couldn't make out. Then his hand moved on her tummy, a caress that made her sigh. She needed to see him, though.

As gracefully as she could, which wasn't very, she moved and shifted until they could look at each other from their respective pillows. His smile told her everything. She hadn't even known she'd been worried, but the relief was real. The night had been real. Given her record on Valentine's Day, that was something of a miracle.

"Good morning," he said.

"Morning."

"I'm glad you're here."

She touched his cheek. "Me too."

"So all that happened, that really did happen?"

She nodded. "Hard to believe, but true."

He just smiled at her, looking sexy with his hair all messed up and his eyes still half-closed. She even liked his five o'clock shadow. It made him look rugged, manly. Edible. But not until she brushed her teeth.

"Why don't you use this bathroom," he said. "Take a shower. It's a great shower."

"What are you going to do?"

"Wait for my turn."

"Hmm," she said, sounding as miffed as she felt.

"What?"

"It's a big shower."

He lifted his head and looked past her to the bedside table. "It's almost nine."

"What does that have to do with anything?"

"It's Tuesday."

"Oh. Yeah. I have a meeting at eleven."

"Which is why we shouldn't shower together."

She moved her hand to his chest, rubbed him right over his nipple, delighted with herself as it got hard under her palm. "We're both mature adults. We can control ourselves."

He glanced down to her hand. "We can?"

She nodded quite seriously.

His hand touched her upper thigh and before she knew it, his fingers were at her entrance. Then slipping inside. "But what if you drop the soap, and I accidentally—"

"Accidentally?"

"It could happen."

She grabbed his wrist as one sneaky finger found her clit. "It's Tuesday."

He frowned. "I have a meeting, too. At ten."

"We need to stop."

His frown deepened. "Fine. We'll stop." He pressed down just hard enough to make her jump. "Five minutes."

She tried to shake her head, but instead relaxed her grip. "We shouldn't."

"Four minutes."

"I have a presentation. I need to…oh."

"You certainly do."

It only took three minutes. She bucked into his hand, whimpered then cried out, shaken. Sated. And still wanting more.

"Of course," he said, letting the words trail. "We could play hooky."

Paige loved the idea, toyed with it for a moment. Especially when he brushed his very hard cock against her thigh. "I'd love to, I really would, but I can't."

He groaned his disappointment.

She lifted her head to stare down at him. "I thought you had a big horrible virus to fight."

Noah grunted. "Stupid computers."

"Terrible things. More trouble than they're worth."

"Damn straight."

She gave him a closed-mouth kiss, then threw back the comforter. "I'll be quick."

"Then I will, too," he said, turning away from her. They both got out of bed. She felt incredible, as if she'd spent a weekend at a spa. Watching him stretch was an added treat, but she didn't dare look below his waist.

"We'll meet back here in fifteen minutes."

"Where will you be?"

"Second bathroom."

"Ah. Okay. Fifteen minutes it is." She hurried to the bathroom, grabbing her overnight bag as she went.

His shower was just as spectacular as she'd imagined. She was careful not to get her hair too wet, and careful not to linger, as much as she'd liked to.

But she did let the water pound her back as she replayed moments from last night. There was still a chance that this was a one-night thing. She didn't want it to be. She couldn't remember the last time she'd been so curious about a man. Curious about everything. His childhood, his work, his friends, his hopes. There was no use calling it anything but what it was: infatuation. He'd swept her off her feet from the moment they'd met.

The first thing she would do when she got to work was call Curt. She would grill him, using force if necessary, to find out if there was any kind of hidden agenda. She prayed there wouldn't be, but with Curt...

It didn't matter, though, did it? She was smitten. She wanted more. Not just to work with Noah, but to be with him. This felt...different. Aside from the sex, which had been life-altering, there was more going on. She saw herself with him. It could be a colossal mistake, one that would leave her in shreds, but she didn't think so. Noah fitted in her life.

Time. She had to get dressed. Put on some makeup, do her hair. It was late, and they both had work. She hated it, but she got ready. All she wanted to do was crawl back in to that big bed of his.

It was after nine-thirty when she came out of the bathroom. He was standing on the other side of the bed, dressed in jeans and a mauve sweater she instantly wanted to touch.

His grin made her giddy, but there was also something expectant in that smile. His gaze darted to the bed.

Flowers. He'd somehow by some magic brought her flowers. Not an arrangement, nothing so studied. Pink-yellow daisies, purple-white mums and orange-fuchsia dahlias. A breath of spring in February.

"What's this?"

"Happy Valentine's Day," he said.

Her mouth opened, but she couldn't think what to say. "But how?" she asked, finally.

"State secret."

"You have a green house?"

"No. But my neighbor does."

"Are you going to be in trouble?"

He nodded. "It's worth it."

She gathered the flowers into a rather large bouquet. Sniffed and found a soft, gentle scent. Let herself shiver that he'd done this. For her. "Thank you," she whispered.

He walked around to her, lifted the flowers from her arms and tossed them once more on the bed. He gathered her close. Kissed her, a long, languid, peppermint-flavored kiss that curled her toes. When he pulled back, he looked at her in that way of his. "I want more. I hope to hell you do, too."

She smiled. "More sounds perfect."

"Perhaps we could start with dinner tonight?"

She kissed him again, rubbed her hands over that delicious sweater, then underneath. The best Valentine's Day ever.

\* \* \* \* \*

## COMING NEXT MONTH

### Available February 22, 2011

**#597 FACE-OFF**
*Encounters*
Nancy Warren

**#598 IN THE LINE OF FIRE**
*Uniformly Hot!*
Jennifer LaBrecque

**#599 IN GOOD HANDS**
Kathy Lyons

**#600 INEVITABLE**
*Forbidden Fantasies*
Michelle Rowen

**#601 HIGH OCTANE**
*Texas Hotzone*
Lisa Renee Jones

**#602 PRIMAL CALLING**
Jillian Burns

# REQUEST YOUR FREE BOOKS!
## 2 FREE NOVELS PLUS 2 FREE GIFTS!

### red-hot reads!

USA TODAY *bestselling author Lynne Graham*
*is back with a thrilling new trilogy*
SECRETLY PREGNANT, CONVENIENTLY WED

*Three heroines must marry alpha males to keep
their dreams…but Alejandro, Angelo and Cesario
are not about to be tamed!*

*Book 1—JEMIMA'S SECRET*
*Available March 2011 from Harlequin Presents®.*

JEMIMA yanked open a drawer in the sideboard to find Alfie's birth certificate. Her son was her husband's child. It was a question of telling the truth whether she liked it or not. She extended the certificate to Alejandro.

"This has to be nonsense," Alejandro asserted.

"Well, if you can find some other way of explaining how I managed to give birth by that date and Alfie not be yours, I'd like to hear it," Jemima challenged.

Alejandro glanced up, golden eyes bright as blades and as dangerous. "All this proves is that you must still have been pregnant when you walked out on our marriage. It does not automatically follow that the child is mine."

"'I know it doesn't suit you to hear this news now and I really didn't want to tell you. But I can't lie to you about it. Someday Alfie may want to look you up and get acquainted."

"If what you have just told me is the truth, if that little boy does prove to be mine, it was vindictive and extremely selfish of you to leave me in ignorance!"

Jemima paled. "When I left you, I had no idea that I was still pregnant."

"Two years is a long period of time, yet you made no attempt to inform me that I might be a father. I will want DNA tests to confirm your claim before I make any decision about what I want to do."

"Do as you like," she told him curtly. "*I* know who Alfie's father is and there has never been any doubt of his identity."

"I will make arrangements for the tests to be carried out and I will see you again when the result is available," Alejandro drawled with lashings of dark Spanish masculine reserve.

"I'll contact a solicitor and start the divorce," Jemima proffered in turn.

Alejandro's eyes narrowed in a piercing scrutiny that made her uncomfortable. "It would be foolish to do anything before we have that DNA result."

"I disagree," Jemima flashed back. "I should have applied for a divorce the minute I left you!"

Alejandro quirked an ebony brow. "And why didn't you?"

Jemima dealt him a fulminating glance but said nothing, merely moving past him to open her front door in a blunt invitation for him to leave.

"I'll be in touch," he delivered on the doorstep.

*What is Alejandro's next move? Perhaps rekindling their marriage is the only solution! But will Jemima agree?*

*Find out in Lynne Graham's
exciting new romance
JEMIMA'S SECRET*

*Available March 2011
from Harlequin Presents®.*

# Start your Best Body today with these top 3 nutrition tips!

1. **SHOP THE PERIMETER OF THE GROCERY STORE:** The good stuff— fruits, veggies, lean proteins and dairy—always line the outer edges of the store. When you veer into the center aisles, you enter the temptation zone, where the unhealthy foods live.

2. **WATCH PORTION SIZES:** Most portion sizes in restaurants are nearly twice the size of a true serving and at home, it's easy to "clean your plate." Use these easy serving guidelines:
   - Protein: the palm of your hand
   - Grains or Fruit: a cup of your hand
   - Veggies: the palm of two open hands

3. **USE THE RAINBOW RULE FOR PRODUCE:** Your produce drawers should be filled with every color of fruits and vegetables. The greater the variety, the more vitamins and other nutrients you add to your diet.

Find these and many more helpful tips in

## YOUR BEST BODY NOW
by
## TOSCA RENO
WITH STACY BAKER

Bestselling Author of
**THE EAT-CLEAN DIET®**

*Available wherever books are sold!*

## HARLEQUIN *Presents*

USA TODAY *Bestselling Author*

# *Lynne Graham*

*is back with her most exciting trilogy yet!*

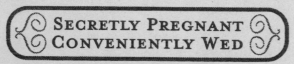

## SECRETLY PREGNANT
## CONVENIENTLY WED

Jemima, Flora and Jess aren't looking for love,
but all have babies very much in mind...and they may
just get their wish and more with the wealthiest, most
handsome and impossibly arrogant men in Europe!

Coming March 2011
# JEMIMA'S SECRET

Alejandro Navarro Vasquez has long desired vengeance after
his wife, Jemima, betrayed him. When he discovers the
whereabouts of his runaway wife—and that she has a two-
year-old son—Alejandro is determined to settle the score....

## FLORA'S DEFIANCE (April 2011)
## JESS'S PROMISE (May 2011)

Available exclusively from Harlequin Presents.

**www.eHarlequin.com**

HP12975